Murder by the Sea

Annette Siketa

Murder by the Sea

FICTION4ALL

Prologue

(I)

"Upper Markham! Upper Markham in two minutes!" Had the tinny, disembodied voice on the public address system, announced that every passenger on the train was to receive the latest mobile phone for free, the ensuing din could not have been louder.

The late burst of summer weather had tempted suburbanites out of their homes, and the carriage was packed with noisy children and their seemingly deaf parents. All were of one mind - to worship the sun with buckets and spades, beach balls and large umbrellas, and enough food to feed a small country for a year.

Alistair Walsh reluctantly glanced out of the window. Fact notwithstanding that the approaching seaside vista did not fill him with joy, the screaming ménage of excited children had given him a headache. To add to his woes, the swaying of the carriage as the train began to slow down made his stomach feel queasy.

***

Alistair was a lawyer. The sedate preciseness of Lady Justice, juxtaposed with the thrust and parry of the courtroom, had appealed from an early age. It still appealed after 25 years at the bar, but not for the reason anyone might have supposed.

5

When Alistair was in his early 40's, someone had made the remark that he bore a striking resemblance to the British actor, Alistair Sim. This had prompted the lawyer to enter the world of amateur dramatics. But, roles were fleeting at best, and his last appearance on stage was in a Christmas play in which his short, portly figure had filled a pumpkin costume to perfection.

His thwarted theatrical ambition saw him turn the courtroom into a 'stage', where every appearance became a 'performance'. Though there was no doubting his brilliance as an advocate, he would never have made an American-style 'TV Judge', primarily because his courtroom dramatics were a cringing mix of Perry Mason, Errol Flynn, and Daffy Duck.

**

The disembodied voice spoke again. "Upper Markham, Upper Markham. All change please. Check the screens for onward connections. All change please."

The ensuing scream of delight that ran through the carriage would have put a jet engine to shame. Taking a steadying breath, Alistair snapped his briefcase shut and prepared to disembark from the train.

Stepping into the aisle, he was almost knocked over by two boys who seemed determined to reach the door before anyone else. Close on their heels was a big woman in a large straw-hat and floral print dress, her exposed, pale flabby arms resembling uncooked legs of lamb.

"Sorry, love," she panted. "If I don't keep up with those two, the little buggers will steal the sand." She ran a critical eye over Alistair's smart three-piece suit. "Bit overdressed for a day at the seaside, aren't you?"

"I am here to meet a client," he answered somewhat stiffly.

"Poor you. Fancy working on a day like today."

"Um…yes, thank you." Alistair had no desire to be rude, but now that the train had stopped, the temperature inside the carriage was beginning to rise. "Ought you to be reclaiming your sons?"

"Oh, blimey," she said with a hearty chuckle, the rolls of fat around her neck wobbling like jelly. "I'll be forgetting me 'ead next." Alistair gave her a quick wan smile and courteously stepped aside.

***

The platform was stifling. Alistair looked longingly at the train. Only a few hours and he could be back in London. Not only that, but now that the steel dragon had regurgitated its cargo, the return journey would be relatively quiet.

He thought of his comfortable air-conditioned office, and not for the first time since leaving King's Cross Station, he asked himself why he had agreed to meet his client, a Miss Davenport, in the seaside hotel where she resided. There were two answers - both of equal importance. Firstly, because she was potentially worth millions, and secondly, because there was a distinct possibility she was in danger.

Extracting his ticket from his waistcoat pocket, Alistair noticed that the platform was deserted, as though every vestige of humanity had suddenly been swept away. To reassure himself that he was not the proverbial 'last man standing', he looked at the beach a short distance away.

And there they were, the suburban hoards worshiping their sun god, the flaccid bodies liberally coated in ritualistic oil. Alistair shuddered. Nothing short of a nuclear holocaust would ever have induced him to join them.

As he walked towards the exit, the first bead of perspiration ran down his back. There was no attendant present. Alistair shrugged, returned his ticket to his waistcoat, and set off to find his client.

Miss Davenport had told him that The Seabridge Hotel was 'just a short walk from the station'. Unfortunately, she had not given precise directions, and so Alistair had little choice but to follow in the wake of the hoards.

Ignoring a plethora of dubious smells, Alistair traversed a litter strewn tunnel that led to a car park and the foreshore. However, any gratitude he may have felt for the brief respite from the sun was short lived, for apart from a large green skip overflowing with rubbish, the car park was empty. With no idea of which direction to take, he doubled back and knocked on the ticket window.

There was no reply, but a radio broadcast of a cricket match, followed by a groan as someone was bowled out, suggested the reason why the attendant had not been present to collect or inspect the tickets.

Alistair knocked again. The window was opened by a middle-aged man with heavy jowls and the affability of the plague. "Yeah? What do you want?" He stopped short when he noticed Alistair's business suit. "Oh, sorry, sir. I thought you were one of those annoying day-trippers. What can I do for you?"

Even though Alistair secretly agreed with the man's description, had they been in court, he would have torn strips off the attendant for the 'politically incorrect' remark. It was a matter of principal. The day-tripping hoards had paid their fare and were entitled to equal consideration.

Alistair opened his briefcase and extracted a notebook. "I am looking for either The Seabridge Hotel, or a shop called Osborne's." When the man looked blank, Alistair added, "I believe it is a haberdashery shop."

A look of comprehension came into the attendant's eyes. "Oh, yes, I know the one. Well, it will take you a good twenty minutes to walk to the hotel, but Osborne's is just around the corner."

Alistair groaned. So much for Miss Davenport's 'short walk'. "Taxi?" he asked hopefully.

The man made a sucking noise through his teeth. "Not on a day like today, sir. It's the hot weather you see. Every taxi service will be stretched to the limit. I can ring up if you like, but you might have to wait an hour or more."

Alistair considered his options. The idea of dodging ice cream splattered children or sweaty people was far from appealing. On the other hand, Miss Davenport did say that she went to the haberdashers every Saturday afternoon. But, would a frail old lady go out on such a hot day?

"May I use your phone?" he asked. "It would be pointless to walk to the hotel only to find that my client is not there." To bolster his request, he 'borrowed' from the woman on the train. "As you can see, I am not dressed for a day at the beach."

The attendant nodded, shut the window, and opened the door. At once, Alistair was blasted with cool air from a fan. He resisted the temptation to remove his jacket and tie. Always a 'snappy' dresser, to him, exposing his sweat-stained shirt was unseemly.

He picked up the phone and dialled the hotel. A man in a singsong voice answered, "Good afternoon, Seabridge Hotel."

Alistair winced. The last thing he needed was sugary exuberance. "Good afternoon. May I speak to Miss Mirabelle Davenport?"

The male voice sounded surprised. "Miss Davenport? I'm sorry but she's out. May I take a message?"

"Have you any idea where she is or when she'll return?"

When the man hesitated, it occurred to Alistair that, for privacy reasons, the hotel would not divulge any information. He therefore flexed his legal muscles. "My name is Alistair Walsh, and I'm her solicitor in London. Only, I'm not in London at the moment. I am calling from the Upper Markham railway station."

The man from the hotel sounded satisfied. "Oh, I see. Well, I don't know where she is at the moment, but she's usually in the hotel around 4.30 for afternoon tea."

Alistair checked his watch. It was just after two o'clock. "I have a second location I can try - a shop called Osborne's. I'll go there now and if she's not there I'll come to the hotel. If she returns in the interim, please tell her that I'll be there shortly."

"I understand. I'll let her know. Goodbye."

The station attendant provided directions, and at Alistair's request, a glass of water. As he drank the barely cool liquid, he pictured his lounge room and his 1930's cocktail cabinet, which was allegedly used as a stage prop in a first-run Noel Coward play.

***

Alistair opened the door to the haberdashers. He could not suppress his relief when he saw his client standing by the counter. "Miss Davenport," he gushed, "thank goodness I found you. I quite dreaded…"

His voice trailed away. He had only met his client once before - all subsequent communication being by telephone, and now he was confronted with two elderly ladies who, apart from a slight difference in height, might have been identical twins. Even their tortoise-shell glasses were the same.

11

Alistair was saved from embarrassment when the real Miss Davenport spoke up. "Why, Mr Walsh, what on earth are you doing here?"

"I'm sorry to intrude into your leisure time, but it is vital that I speak to you privately. I rang the hotel, but the man who answered said you were out."

"That would have been the ubiquitous Mr Ayres," she responded tartly. "But, how did you know I would be here?"

"During our discussions on the phone, you mentioned that you sometimes came here on a Saturday afternoon to, as you put it, 'peruse the pattern books'."

Miss Davenport sounded impressed. "How clever of you to remember. Oh, how remiss of me. This is my good friend, Elizabeth Wilson. She also resides at the hotel."

Manners dictated that Alistair should shake hands, but as his palms were hot and sweaty, he felt awkward about performing the act of civility. He now employed his hitherto undiscovered acting ability, whereby under the pretext of adjusting his briefcase, he covertly wiped his hand on his trousers. But the charade was not necessary, for Elizabeth Wilson was wearing gloves.

The act thus performed, Alistair addressed his client again. "Forgive my abruptness but I cannot stay long. Is there somewhere nearby where we can talk privately?"

Elizabeth Wilson emitted a discrete cough. "I'll leave you in peace." She turned and addressed the young woman behind the counter. "Caroline, my dear, please let me know at once when the wool arrives."

Caroline McGuiness smiled deferentially. How she would have loved to tell the old lady where to stick the wool. But, autumn would soon be on the doorstep, driving the tourists into hibernation. Consequently, it would not do to offend such a regular customer.

Of the two old ladies, Caroline preferred Miss Davenport. Not that there was anything wrong with Elizabeth Wilson. It was just that she had a habit of playing annoying jokes, such as the time she put sneezing powder in a basket of potpourri.

"Well, goodbye," said Elizabeth, and with a regal wave of her hand she exited the shop.

"Mr Walsh," said Miss Davenport, "there's a cafe around the corner." She looked slightly embarrassed as she added, "I'm afraid it bears no resemblance to anything we would have been accustomed to in our youth."

Alistair inclined his head. "Anywhere will do."

She turned to Caroline. "Would you mind if I left my purchases here? I'll pick them up later."

Caroline gave her a genuine smile. "Not at all, but please remember that we close at 4.30 today. If you're not back by then, I'll pop up to the hotel in the morning and leave them at the reception desk."

"Thank you, my dear." Miss Davenport removed her glasses and put them in her handbag. "This way, Mr Walsh."

As Caroline watched them walk up the street, she was struck by how comfortable they seemed together. Miss Davenport was doing all the talking,

13

while Mr Walsh was listening attentively, occasionally nodding his head. Rather than client and solicitor, they looked more like Aunt and Nephew.

Caroline was about to turn away when she suddenly frowned. She had just seen someone who, in the normal course of events, should not have been there. "Now, I wonder what he's doing in this neck of the woods," she murmured. "I haven't seen him up here in ages." She shrugged. "Oh well, I'll ask him when I see him later."

Turning away from the window, her gaze fell on a display of old-fashioned doilies, which had been placed on the counter as a 'special'. The shop had been established when grace and propriety were commonplace, and Mrs Osborne, the third generation owner, sold products that modern society now deemed quaint.

To Caroline however, the shop was more like a museum, and a new redevelopment project that included two state-of-the-art supermarkets, was like a red rag to a bull. If she could secure a position in one of the new shops, even if it was only stacking shelves, she could escape the dryness of the past. She might even find a little excitement.

Sighing in lament, she opened a shipment of embroidery thread and attacked them with a pricing gun.

(II)

Sergeant Harry Briggs stood up and removed his latex gloves. "Definitely dead, sir."

"I see all those years of training haven't gone to waste," replied Inspector Butler dryly. "What gave it away? The fact that he's as stiff as a board or the gaping hole in his head? Do we know who he is?"

Sergeant Briggs ignored the sarcasm. "Apart from a return train ticket to London in his waistcoat pocket, he was picked clean."

The Inspector glanced at the Upper Markham railway sign. "As we're not in the car park at an airport, a train ticket is hardly surprising. Anything else?"

"His suit was made in London. An exclusive label I'd say, so we might be able to trace him through the tailor."

Inspector Raymond Butler shuddered. A veteran of the force, much of his early service had been spent with the 'Met', and yet he hated London with a passion. Nothing short of receiving a knighthood at the palace would ever induce him to return. London might only be a couple of hours away, but as far as he was concerned, it was on another planet, and what's more, it could stay there.

He studied the as yet unidentified body of Alistair Walsh. "He looks like a bank manager or an accountant. I wonder where his briefcase is."

Sergeant Briggs raised an eyebrow. "How do you know he had a briefcase?"

It was a perfectly reasonable question, and yet it irritated the Inspector. It had been a long 24 hours for the Upper Markham Constabulary, and nobody was at their sparkling best.

"Look at his clothes, man. You don't come out for a day at the seaside dressed in a three piece suit."

"True," agreed the sergeant. "Any news on the other body?"

Inspector Butler arched his back. He was short of sleep, short of manpower, and short of caffeine. "Nope, but at least we know the name - Mirabelle Davenport." He paused and then added thoughtfully, "I wonder which of them died first."

"Does it matter?"

"No idea, but my copper's instinct is telling me that two brutal deaths in 24 hours is not a coincidence."

Chapter 1. Three Months Later.

It was Sunday when Florrie spotted the advert. The unpretentious listing appeared in a special newspaper feature entitled, 'End of Season Holiday Bargains', and stated that The Seabridge Hotel was 'quiet and comfortable', that it catered for 'long and short term guests', and that it would 'suit persons of gentility'. In point of fact, the proprietors of the hostelry had been running the advert since the 1960's and had never found cause to change the wording.

Before announcing the find, and with the finesse of a 50-year-old vacuum cleaner, Florrie cleared a lump of masticated biscuit from under the top palette of her false teeth. "Listen to this, Ada, it's just what the doctor ordered." She read the advert aloud, but due to the absence of her new glasses, pronounced the last word as 'gentry'.

Mrs Ada Harris did not need to be a Rhodes Scholar or a professor of English to know that her friend had made a mistake. She retrieved the newspaper and read the advert for herself.

"That's gentility, not gentry. Silly old fool. You made it sound like a retirement home for ageing peers of the realm. I do wish you'd wear your new reading glasses."

"And I wish I'd kept my old ones," replied Florrie, grumpily.

***

As a plethora of shop owners, supermarket assistants, and bus conductors could attest, Mrs Florence Brown, or Florrie to her friends, could be infuriatingly stubborn. However, when she was almost fined for trying to use a library card as a bus pass, she had reluctantly agreed to an eye test.

The result was to say the least, mixed. Whilst her eyesight had not degenerated too much with age, the glasses were another matter. In a parody of the infamous Judge Jefferies, who had a habit of finding defendants guilty even though they were innocent, the optician had announced that the old frame was too brittle to support modern glass, at which point the glasses were transported to the rubbish bin for life.

Florrie had protested vociferously, but no appeal or victim impact statement was considered. The optometrist had then selected a new frame, claiming that the style would match Florrie's character. However, when she returned to collect the new glasses, her shriek of horror could have been heard outside the shop.

"I look like a frog! I'll never be able to show my face in public again."

The black horn rimmed frame dominated her face, and the thick tinted glass magnified her green eyes, thus making them appear protuberant. Unfortunately, the reptilian effect had been enhanced due to the fact that she was wearing a green dress at the time.

Ada, who had witnessed the great unveiling, tried to hide her amusement by saying, "Oh, stop complaining. You don't look the least batrachian."

But rather than calming Florrie's ire, the remark had prompted her to vent a long-standing complaint. "I hate it when you use perky words." Her response was perhaps a little hypocritical, for 'perky' was her own slang for 'peculiar'.

"Batrachian," explained Ada, "means anything frog-like in appearance. You should be grateful. At least you won't be receiving any more letters from the bus company."

Since then, the glasses had not seen much service, and as Florrie scowled and jerked the newspaper, she trotted out her now familiar excuse for their non-appearance.

"I left them at home. It's not my fault if newspapers are printed in a much smaller font nowadays. No wonder everything's going online. I do wish you'd get a computer."

Ada burst out laughing. "The font size hasn't changed in years, and as for a computer, I am a complete technophobe."

"Nonsense. You know how to use a microwave and a food processor and you can set an alarm clock. It's simply a matter of application."

Florrie had taken to the Internet like a duck to water, and was always coming out with strange facts and trivia, such as the fate of J. Murray Spangler, who at the turn of the 19th century, invented a device he called the 'electric suction sweeper'.

Unable to sell the device commercially, he turned for advice to W. H. Hoover, a leather goods maker, who knew nothing about electric devices but recognised the potential of the invention. Hoover became rich and famous whereas Spangler was lost to history.

"Well," said Ada, "go and apply yourself to the kitchen and make a fresh pot of tea." She picked up a small brown bottle from the table by her chair. "Time for this useless medication."

Though the remark was flippant, the underlying premise gave Florrie cause for thought. A week or so earlier, Ada had injured her hip whilst visiting one of her innumerable relatives. She had returned home in an ambulance, and her explanation that she'd fallen down some steps had not sat well with Florrie. In fact, she'd been downright suspicious, and not without reason.

*   *   *

Ada and Florrie had been friends for nearly 60 years. They had met at school when, through silliness and exuberance, they'd accidentally banged their heads together. Following this 'meeting of the minds' as Ada later described it, their teenage years were a mirror image - the same style of clothing, the same hobbies and taste in music, and the same plethora of adolescent complaints.

Ada had been fair haired, rather dumpy, and susceptible to pimples, whereas Florrie had been svelte, pale-skinned, and with long, thick, glossy black hair. She might have had a career as a model had she not been flat chested. The missing appendages did finally appear, but not until the birth of her first child.

After leaving school, Ada and Florrie had become 'dailies' or 'char women'. This was due more to a lack of opportunities than education, not that either woman minded, for there was plenty of work to be had.

Unfortunately, Florrie's introduction to the adult world had been a baptism of fire, for being young and attractive but far from naive, she had been forced to fight off randy husbands' and similar clients - and not all of them male.

At age 22, Florrie married Edward 'Ted' Brown, with Ada following a year later to Frank Harris. Ted Brown was charming and resourceful and considered a prized catch. However, the honeymoon had barely ended when he revealed his true colours.

He was a wastrel and a drunkard, and his so-called resourcefulness was nothing but dodgy dealing. He was constantly on the scrounge, sinking money into 'get rich quick' schemes, no matter how improbable or ludicrous.

His recklessness had twice landed him in prison, and as a consequence, Florrie had become adept at cooking on an open fire. This had nothing to do with camping or outdoor pursuits, but rather, with no money to pay the bills, the electricity had been cut off.

By the time she turned 25, Florrie had looked ten years older. A physical and mental wreck, her exhaustion had been exacerbated by the birth of three children in quick succession. Then, on a bitterly cold winter evening, everything had changed.

21

Ted had already demonstrated his propensity to speak with his fists, and when he stole his children's Christmas present money to sink into yet another dodgy scheme, it was the final straw. A violent argument ensued, and after enduring yet another beating, Florrie had grabbed her children and fled.

The Harris's lived in the next street, and when Ada had opened her front door, she had barely recognised her friend. Florrie's face was covered in bruises, and one lip was split and swollen. Having created the impression that nothing was wrong in the marriage, Florrie had broken down and confessed the truth.

Later that night after Florrie and her children had been safely ensconced in Ada's spare bedroom, 'certain wheels' had been put in motion. Ted Brown had been arrested the following day and charged with assault and battery. Given his criminal record, plus a confidential note sent to the magistrate by a certain government official, Ted was sent to prison for ten years.

Florrie never saw him again, and over the following decades, she and Ada observed the brutality of apartheid, the pointless Vietnam war, and the assassination of John F. Kennedy. On the bright side, they witnessed the blossoming of the young Queen Elizabeth II, the moon landings, and given their profession, the evolution of arguably the most labour saving device ever invented - the washing machine.

By the late 1980's, Ada and Florrie's respective families were well established, with five children and seven grandchildren between them. The bulk of

Mrs Brown's family resided in America, while Ada's 'brood' as she affectionately called them, were scattered across Australia.

The passage of time had left its mark. Florrie's once statuesque figure had acquired the stoop of the aged, and her once luxuriant thick black hair was now a mop of white curls. Conversely, the now widowed Ada had blossomed into a typical roly-poly grandma, with twinkling blue eyes and chubby pink cheeks. She kept her silver grey hair short and tidy, though every now and then she allowed herself the indulgence of a perm.

It was testament to their ability and vast experience that, even though near retirement age, both were still employed, albeit part-time. Mrs Brown worked three days a week as a cleaner for the local council, while Ada did occasional jobs for the 'Clean 4U Agency', which somewhat curiously, was not listed in the phone book.

Yet despite their enduring friendship, something had nagged at Mrs Brown for years, namely, that there was a part of her best friend's life that had been kept hidden. Florrie had no actual evidence for her suspicion, rather, it was a gut feeling based on the décor of Ada's home.

Two painted tribal wooden masks, complete with boned nose and jagged teeth, stared down from a wall, whilst above the doorway, two razor-sharp Turkish scimitars encircled a bronze-age axe. An ancient Egyptian mummified cat sat proudly on the mantelpiece, while a Native American Indian headdress was displayed fan-like on the chimneybreast. The long mahogany sideboard strained under the weight of statues and figurines, and the china cabinet was crammed so full that the mirror backing hadn't reflected the sun in years.

Another curious item was tucked in a corner and partially hidden by the TV. It was a full sized, exquisitely engraved Russian samovar. Unfortunately, a small round hole in the base rendered it inoperative, and so it now displayed an attractive mix of peacock feathers and ferns.

It seemed every country was represented, and many of the items were connected to Frank Harris. He had been a happy, friendly man, with a joke or a truism for just about every occasion. Being an engineer, he would sometimes spend days or even weeks away from home. But, had he really been in Manchester or Edinburgh as claimed, or had he been somewhere else?

Florrie clearly remembered when Frank had walked through the door carrying the mummified cat. He was supposed to have been working in Egypt, but he later stated that he'd bought the relic on the 'black market' in Germany. The discrepancy might have been pardonable had Ada not later declared the location to be Holland.

This had been the first of several slip-up's that, on the surface, seemed innocuous. And yet they had all stuck in Florrie's mind, as had the arrest of her husband. Justice had certainly worked swiftly, and yet she, Florrie, had not made a complaint to the police. Had Frank and Ada been involved with...whatever they were involved with, all those years ago? Indeed, rather than falling down some steps, was there another reason behind Ada's hip injury?

Shaking off her reverie, Florrie returned to the subject of the 'useless medicine'. "Ha! And you have the cheek to call me a silly old fool. That doctor this morning? His mutton-chop sideburns and patched hacking jacket reminded me of a 1960's country vet. It wouldn't have surprised me if he'd prescribed worming tablets."

"Or a shot for distemper," quipped Ada, who agreed with the characterisation.

"And what about his so-called medical advice?" Florrie pulled a face and mimicked the doctor's Scottish brogue. In spite of her cockney origin, she was very good at imitating accents. "'You need to rest your leg as much as possible. Get away for a while- the country or the seaside perhaps. Sometimes the old remedies are the best' - that'll be £55 thank you very much. Huh! I noticed his prices weren't old-fashioned. What did you have to go to a private doctor for?"

Laughing uproariously, Ada deftly sidestepped the question. "At least we won't need to traipse around travel agents for possible destinations."

"True. Nice of the newspaper to print that special feature. I bet that's where Doc Mutton-Chops got the idea for your cure."

"In that case," said Ada, quickly scanning the adverts again, "he must have thought I was much younger than I look. Listen to this - 'More pleasure for your pound in Portugal'. Or how about this - 'Visit Spain - where the days are hot and the nights even hotter'." She gave a small sniff of disapproval.

"Spain? At my age? What nonsense. I can really see a night of flamenco dancing improving the state of my hip."

"Oh, I don't know," said Florrie with a rakish grin. "I can just picture you in a sombrero. A nice big floppy one made of straw." She ran a critical eye around the room. "It's about the only thing you ain't got in here."

"There's not enough room," replied Ada flippantly, though the pointed remark was not lost on her. She returned to the adverts again. "By comparison, The Seabridge Hotel sounds positively sedate. Yes, I think it will do very nicely."

"Do you want any supper?" asked Florrie, moving towards the kitchen.

"Just something light," replied Ada, picking up the phone. She dialled the hotel and was soon chatting to a Mr Ayres as though he was a long lost cousin.

Florrie listened for a moment and was not surprised at her friend's 'gift of the gab'. By asking unobtrusive, almost mundane questions, Ada could usually extract all manner of gossip or private information, even from complete strangers. Florrie had witnessed it enough times to know there was no mysticism or hypnotism involved, and although she'd made several attempts to copy the technique, the results were poor at best.

***

Florrie made scrambled eggs on toast for two, adding her own touch of chopped chives and onions. She completed the repast with a pot of hot strong tea. She watched a soap opera, two game shows, and the ten o'clock news, after which she washed the dishes and went home. Had she still been in the lounge room 15 minutes later when the phone rang, all her suspicions regarding her friend would have been validated at once.

Ada used the remote control to turn off the TV. Given the time difference between England and Australia, she was not unduly alarmed at receiving a late night call. However, it was not whom she thought it might be.

"Oh, hello, Bert. You're working late." Ada listened attentively to the softly spoken voice. "Well, what a coincidence, I've just booked in there for a few days. I suppose I could have a poke around, after all, I've a legitimate reason for being there. Just a moment, Bert."

Retrieving her voluminous handbag, she extracted a notebook and pen. Then, amidst shopping lists, recipes, and things to remember, she wrote in a language that anyone would have regarded as gibberish.

A few minutes later she replaced the receiver. The 'job' she had been given was not particularly difficult. On the contrary, compared to some of the tasks she'd tackled in the past, it could almost be described as mundane. The problem, as she knew from experience, was that the solution might already have been 'swept away'.

Chapter 2. The Seabridge Hotel.

With suitcase and walking stick in hand, Ada alighted from the train at Upper Markham railway station. Though the sun was shining, a cool breeze blowing off the ocean was a reminder that autumn had arrived. She joined the trickle of passengers heading for the exit, barely glancing at the closed ticket window.

She walked through the short viaduct that led to the car park. Seagulls screamed over her head, and the tangy smell of salty air filled her nostrils. She looked around as if searching for someone who was supposed to be meeting her. Then, adopting an expression of disappointment, she approached a taxi parked by a wall.

"Are you available?" she asked politely.

"Certainly." The driver jumped out and opened the rear door. "Where to?"

"The Seabridge Hotel."

Being mindful of her hip, which was still giving her trouble, she slid into the car and shut the door. The driver, an elderly man with a face the colour and texture of withered parchment, put the suitcase in the boot and climbed behind the wheel again.

"Would you like to go directly or take the scenic route?"

"What's the difference?"

"About 10 seconds!"

As the driver guffawed at his own joke, Ada doubted this was the first time he'd uttered the response. Nevertheless, she smiled in amusement and matched his mood. After all, one never knew when a 'speedy' friend might be needed.

"Oh, let's be daring and hang the expense."

He started the engine and whether by accident or design, shot out of the car park. The tyres screeched like souls in torment as the taxi turned sharp right, narrowly missing the pavement and two cyclists who had stopped to look at the sea.

If he was aware that his driving would have been more at home in Indianapolis or Imola, he gave no sign as he asked, "Are you here on holiday?"

The manoeuvre had literally tossed Ada across the back seat. She collected her wits and straightened her slewed hat. "Yes," she answered, now clinging to her seatbelt with a grip of iron. "I saw an advert in the paper, and as I've never been here before, I thought I'd come and take a look."

"Well, make sure it's a good one cos the place won't be the same next year. You see those?" He pointed to the right, where tall yellow bollards blocked off large tracts of land. Had it not been for the artfully designed letter 'T' prominently displayed on each, the garish fencing might have been mistaken for a modern-day sculpture.

The sun reflecting off the yellow paint was eye watering. Ada could only manage a quick look before turning away. "What are they doing?" she asked.

"It's a massive redevelopment project," he explained. "The council wants to turn Upper Markham into an English version of the Costa del

Sol. If me old dad was still alive, he'd be kicking himself black & blue."

"Why?"

"Because he once had the chance of buying a house right here on the front. Me brothers and I were in short pants at the time, and we were really excited about living so close to the beach.

"But, me old dad knocked it back, saying that there would be problems with salt damage, and so he bought a house a few streets away instead."

Ada perceived the inference at once. "Which, had he bought the first house, would now be worth a tidy sum."

"Exactly." He gestured through the windscreen to a point in the distance. "Up there is the old part of town. If you get the chance, visit the pier. The whole area's being flattened.

"The developers have paid a fortune for the houses, though I admit some of 'em were eyesores, and those who refused to sell were slapped with a council compulsory purchase order."

"What's being built?"

The driver grunted. "You name it – shops, apartments, supermarkets."

"I take it you don't approve."

"No. Upper Markham mightn't be much, but it's a sleepy sort of place where everybody knows just about everybody else. When the development was first proposed, some of the residents formed an action group. Bloody pointless. It would have been easier to stop the waves from rolling on the beach."

Just then, the taxi came to a sudden stop. "Here you are, missus - the Seabridge Hotel."

He retrieved the suitcase from the boot. Ada paid him and included a good tip. In return, he presented her with his business card. "Just ring if you need me." He jumped into the taxi and sped away, leaving his passenger to contemplate her temporary home.

Though Ada had not been expecting anything fancy, her first impression was less than favourable. Four storeys high with a façade of weatherworn red brick, the portico would have been impressive had it not been suffering from neglect.

The intricate curlicue white iron railings, which stretched between two front columns and the walls, were dotted with rust and flaky paint, while the six scuffed marble steps were in desperate need of a good scrubbing.

Ada entered the hotel and was immediately greeted by the sight of two elderly ladies confronting a man behind the reception desk. The assessment of hostility had nothing to do with second sight or prophecy, but rather, that one of the ladies was shaking an umbrella in his face.

Her ¾ length thick black coat would have fetched a king's ransom in any antique clothing shop, and her squat black hat had a bunch of imitation cherries pinned to the side. Had the umbrella been fashioned with a parrot-head handle, her outfit would have matched the costume worn by Julie Andrews in 'Mary Poppins'.

But that's where the resemblance to the loveable nanny ended, for the voice was what Florrie would have called 'a plum in the mouth posh accent'. Indeed, with her crisp pronunciation and

31

emphasised vowels, if the old lady had been wearing a smart beige suit and an obscenely overpriced hat, she could have passed for a duchess in the royal box at Ascot.

Altilioquent thought Ada, and scrutinised the second lady, who was half a head shorter than her companion. Dressed in a Macintosh and a limp straw hat, had she been shod in gumboots, she might have been a farmer's wife who'd come to town for the day.

The illusion of agricultural domesticity was spoilt by her shuffling feet and downcast, faded blue eyes, which seemed to convey the message, 'I wish I was anywhere else but here'. Her embarrassment was understandable, for her friend was speaking volubly and with very little tact.

"Mr Ayres, these insidious practical jokes must cease immediately." Her voice rose several octaves as she emphatically stated, "Either he goes - or we do!"

"Elizabeth, I don't think Mr Ayres is ignorant of the problem," said the second old lady. Her voice, unlike the aristocratic stateliness of her friend, sounded like a twittering bird. "I'm quite sure he's doing everything to stop them."

Ignoring her friend's attempt at pacification, 'Mary Poppins' spoke with undisguised contempt. "Well, I am not. His efforts are pathetic at best."

The man in question was round-faced, balding, and in his 60's. He was smartly if casually dressed in dark slacks, a white shirt, and a maroon tie. Solidly built but more from flab than muscle, his grey sleeveless jumper did little to hide his paunch.

He spied the new guest and held out a hand, the effusiveness of his greeting betraying the fact that the old lady had tested his patience. "Ah, you must be Ada. We spoke on the phone. Welcome to the Seabridge Hotel. I am your host and proprietor, Cedric Ayres."

"Thank you," she responded, throwing a conspicuous glance at the old ladies. "I hope I'm not interrupting anything important."

Mr Ayres tried to smile but it lacked sincerity. "Not at all," he said, holding out a registration card. "Just a little in-house misunderstanding."

As Ada took the card, her eyes darted to the ladies again. She was interested to see what impact – if any, his dismissive statement had made. The results spoke for themselves. The second lady now wore an expression that said, 'I wish the ground would open up and swallow me', while 'Mary Poppins' looked as if she'd like to wrap her umbrella around his neck.

Her curiosity satisfied, Ada filled-in the card and handed it back. Mr Ayres read the details and then said, "Five nights as agreed on the phone. Please excuse me while I complete the registration process."

He turned around and stood in front of a rear counter, where two banks of pigeonholes were separated by a square mirror. A large sign above the mirror read, 'Please do not leave the hotel with your key. They are expensive to replace and may be needed in an emergency'.

But the glaringly obvious was missing. "Don't you use a computer?" she asked.

33

"No," he answered, writing in an old-fashioned ledger, "I'm a bit long in the tooth for that sort of thing. I much prefer pen and paper."

In the pause that followed, Ada took in her surroundings. In front of her and to the right of the desk was a door marked 'Private', and beyond that, a dimly lit corridor. The smell of beer indicated that there was a bar at the other end. Behind her were a double set of glass doors, a lift, and a narrow set of carpeted stairs.

The foyer itself was a pseudo-art deco style that interior designers could strive years to achieve. The dark wood half-wall panelling, clashed with the blue paintwork. The chandelier and wall sconces were at odds with the fluorescent lighting above the desk, while the bland grey carpet would have been more at home in an office. The overall impression was that someone had tried to drag the old hotel into the 21st century, and had either run out of money or given up.

Ada could well imagine that in its heyday, the hotel evinced an air of uncomplicated refinement. Ladies in stiff corseted gowns sipped afternoon tea whilst a string quartet played unobtrusively in the background. Nowadays, it was jeans, suntan oil, and Ipods'.

Her nostalgia was interrupted when Mr Ayres rang a small brass bell. A moment later, a young man wearing dark blue trousers, a crisp white shirt, a clip-on 'dickie' bow tie, and a bright red waistcoat, emerged from the dimly lit corridor.

"You rang?" he said, a touch of insolence in his voice.

Mr Ayres barely moved his lips as he replied, "Number 26." He handed the valet a key with a brass nametag before addressing Ada again. "We have a pleasant cocktail lounge if you would like a drink before dinner." He indicated the dimly lit corridor. "And over there," he pointed to the set of glass doors, "is the dining room. We cater to all tastes, and can prepare special meals if you have dietary requirements. Travis here will escort you to your room. Enjoy your stay."

The valet picked up the suitcase and went to the lift. He pressed the button for the second floor, and even before the door slid closed, the animated discussion between the old ladies and Mr Ayres had resumed.

It had not escaped Ada's attention that Mr Ayres and the valet had not made eye contact. Indeed, instead of conveying a 'we are all one big happy family' attitude, the men had resembled two gunfighters just itching to draw their weapons. Clearly there was tension between proprietor and employee.

She had also noticed something else. The only apparent exit was via the foyer door. She supposed there was a rear door in the kitchen, but how many guests would know where to find it? In her 'second' profession, details such as escape routes tended to be rather important.

***

Room 26 was exactly as the advert had stated - quiet and comfortable. To the immediate right was a

35

door to an ensuite, while on the left was a large built-in double wardrobe. The carpet was the same dull grey as in the foyer, while the red damask curtains and bedspread, though clean and respectable, had definitely seen better days. At each side of the double bed was a single-drawed nightstand, with a telephone and glass ashtray on the right. An armchair under the window, a heavy 4-drawer mirrored dressing table, and a long low coffee table that could double as a luggage rack, completed the furnishings.

The valet placed the suitcase on the table. Then, almost in one breath, he recited what was obviously a much repeated monologue. "Soft drinks are free in the cocktail lounge for children aged twelve and under. Breakfast is served in the dining room from 7.00 am to 9.30 am. Luncheon is from 11.30 am to 1.30 pm, with dinner from 6.00 pm to 9.30 pm. Full details are contained in the hotel brochure located in the nightstand."

Ada almost clapped. He had reminded her of a circus seal that had just performed very well. A 'fishy' reward was expected, and she was only too happy to oblige. She extracted several coins from her voluminous handbag, but instead of dropping them into his now outstretched hand, she held them back.

"What practical jokes were the old ladies referring to?"

The valet dropped his eyes and studied his feet. His embarrassment resembled that of a Michelin chef who, despite protesting that his food was always made with the 'freshest ingredients', had been caught using tinned products.

"Um…we have a small group of long-term residents, and every now and then, one of them likes to play practical jokes. I suppose the old boy gets bored and wants to liven things up a bit. It can get rather boring here at times."

When Ada did not respond, the valet, concerned that he might have alarmed her, quickly added, "Nothing hurtful you understand, just silly childish tricks."

Ada was more intrigued than alarmed. "And what did this old boy do to rattle the old ladies?"

Her unconcerned manner and ingratiating smile seemed to put the valet at ease, for he now spoke more freely. "I suppose it was Miss Elizabeth who was doing the complaining."

"If you mean the woman who looks like an aged version of 'Mary Poppins', then yes."

"Thought so. Miss Katherine wouldn't say 'boo' to a goose. But, I suppose Miss Elizabeth had cause to complain. She always has her own copies of the Sunday papers delivered to the hotel, and when they reached her room this morning…well, let's just say that one of the supplement magazines was not the exposé she was expecting."

"Oh, dear," she said with a chuckle, and held out the coins. The valet winked, bowed, and left the room.

After depositing her hat and coat in the wardrobe, Ada opened her suitcase. She removed a toiletries bag and a small collapsible travelling alarm clock. It was rather battered and had a dent on

37

one side, and yet she handled it with the same care as a Faberge egg.

Not only was the clock the first gift Frank had given her after she'd been 'recruited', but it had once saved her life, and as she ran her fingers over the dent, she remembered the Russian ballerina whom she'd helped to defect.

"Sentimental old fool," she murmured, noticing the time. It was nearly five o'clock. She took the toiletry bag into the bathroom, performed a quick wash and brush-up, and then considered the walking stick, which was propped against the bed.

In the foyer, she had simply held the stick in her hand. Indeed, she had brought it more for effect than functionality. But, should she employ it now? Should she present herself as an invalid or a relatively healthy woman for her age?

She decided on the latter, reasoning that it was easier to fake an injury than a recovery. She picked-up her handbag, put the stick in the wardrobe, and then left the room, making sure that the door was properly locked.

Chapter 3. Less Than Friends.

Mr Ayres was not behind the reception desk when Ada crossed the foyer. She entered the cocktail lounge and stopped dead. The fishing nets, anchors, life buoys, steering lights, and every other piece of boating paraphernalia, were as fake as the Hitler diaries.

But this was a minor distraction compared to the bar itself. Someone had tried to re-create a 17th century poop deck, but whether the design was based on a Spanish galleon, a Portuguese man o'war, or an Elizabethan Naval ship, was anyone's guess. Whoever had designed it deserved to be hoisted up the nearest yardarm.

A group of patrons were already seated. On the far side of the room, an impeccably dressed man in his 40's was reading a newspaper. Beside him, a pretty young woman in her 20's was rummaging in a handbag. Two tables across were a couple in their 50's. The man had his nose buried in a book, while his female companion, who was wearing a garish yellow dress, looked utterly bored. The other patrons, most of whom were aged under forty, were either whispering, staring into space, or playing with their mobile phones.

'Mary Poppins' and her companion were sitting in front of the bar. They seemed very interested in a man staring out of the large picture window, for they kept turning their heads and casting unpleasant glances at him. Was this the 'old boy' who liked to play practical jokes? Ada decided to find out.

"Excuse me, ladies," she said politely. "I saw you earlier when I arrived, and as I don't know anyone here, I was wondering if I might join you."

"Certainly," said 'Mary Poppins' affably, and moved her chair to make room for a third. "But I'm afraid you'll have to wait for a drink. The staff are changing shifts. I am Elizabeth Wilson, and this is my sister, Katherine."

Elizabeth was wearing a floral print dress, and Katherine a plain grey skirt and blouse. Apart from a slight resemblance in the nose, there was nothing familial about them. Neither woman was wearing a wedding ring, and nor was there a telltale white mark.

"And I am Ada Harris," she said, and shook the proffered hands. "Do the staff always change shifts at this time of day?"

"This one does," answered Elizabeth, indicating a liveried bartender who had just strolled into the room. If he was aware of expectant eyes watching his every move, he gave no sign as he set to work.

There was not exactly a stampede to the bar. It was more of an orderly rush, and dismissing the sister's protests, Ada did the honours - a whiskey for herself, a small dry sherry for Katherine, and a gin and tonic for Elizabeth.

The drinks were placed on a tray, and resuming her seat, Ada noticed that the man by the window waited until everyone had been served before approaching the bar. He spoke to the barman for a moment or two, and then turned away with half a pint of beer in his hand.

"Good evening, ladies," he said as he passed their table, not looking at anyone in particular.

It was not until he was out of earshot that Elizabeth Wilson spoke her mind. "I know we have only just met, and I do not wish to seem overly familiar, but I advise you to avoid that man at all cost. He is utterly reprehensible and not to be trusted."

Ada raised her glass and peered at him over the rim. "Is that the man you were complaining about to Mr Ayres?"

"Yes. He is a scoundrel, and I have repeatedly asked Mr Ayres to refuse him further accommodation."

Aged in his late 60's or early 70's, the 'scoundrel' was smartly dressed in grey slacks, blue jacket, a white shirt, and a red and blue striped tie. A flat white cap adorned his head, and his thick, 'salt & pepper' moustache had a military bearing.

And yet there was something not quite right about the presented picture, and it took Ada a moment to pin it down. It was his expression. As he stared out of the window, he seemed to emit an air of resignation, as though expecting a friend who, deep in his heart, he knew would never arrive.

Ada pronounced judgement. "He looks harmless to me."

Katherine leaned across the table and spoke in a hushed, slightly breathless voice. "We also thought that at first, but he has a nasty habit of playing jokes on people. You see…"

"That will do," said her sister, firmly. "It would be best to remain silent. We do not want to frighten Ada, especially on her first day."

In spite of the warning, Katherine seemed determined to give her opinion. "Ada should be on her guard. Have you forgotten his involvement in that awful business with Miss Davenport?"

"Katherine!" Elizabeth's sharp retort and withering glare could have cracked an iceberg. It instantly silenced her chattering sister, who shrank back in her chair.

There was a stony silence, and Ada wondered if Elizabeth had been diplomatic, or had Katherine somehow been indiscrete? To avoid the awkwardness impacting on the conversation, Ada asked a mundane question.

"Have you been here long?"

"On and off, about 30 years," replied Elizabeth. "However, I retired from the theatre some six months ago, and we have resided here ever since."

"Twelve months," said Katherine sulkily, clearly still chafing from her sister's rebuke.

Elizabeth Wilson opened her mouth as if to interrupt again, but somewhere between thought and action she seemingly changed her mind. Instead, she twisted her mouth into the semblance of a smile and muttered a curt, "Correct."

It was hardly a ringing endorsement, and once again Ada perceived tension between the sisters. She kept the conversation flowing by saying, "Oh, how marvellous. When I was a young girl at school, I wanted to tread the boards but my voice was not strong enough. What was your speciality? Drama, comedy, or Shakespeare?"

"I suppose technically, all three," answered Elizabeth. "I was a senior wardrobe mistress. I did do a little understudying on occasions, but nothing so grand as to be a leading lady."

Seemingly recovered from her dressing down, Katherine chipped in, "Tell Ada about the famous people you've worked with."

Elizabeth responded with modesty. "Well, yes, I have been fortunate to work with some of the greats, but only in my capacity as a costumier. There was Gielgud of course, and Ustinov - such a charming man. Then there was an actor who, as young as he was at the time, was extraordinarily gifted.

"He went on to scale the heights, and I like to think the little piece of advice I gave him, helped his career. I told him that, no matter what life held in store, he should never forget his roots for they would always keep him grounded. He became a famous movie star, but like many of them from that era, his first love was the theatre."

Ada waited for a moment, and when no name was mentioned, curiosity prompted her to ask, "Who was it?"

In a gesture that echoed the Victorian era, Elizabeth covered her mouth and let out a coquettish titter. "Oh, silly me. It was Richard Burton." Picking up her glass of gin & tonic, she was about to drink when she suddenly stopped. "Goodness me, where is my mind these days? I

43

have forgotten the most important of all, the impresario, the maestro, the one and only - Olivier."

Ada was genuinely impressed. "You worked with Laurence Olivier?"

"Oh, yes," replied Elizabeth, a note of self-importance creeping into her voice. "I had tea with his wife, Miss Vivienne Leigh on several occasions. A lovely girl but rather neurotic, but then, considering the revelations after her husband's death, perhaps this is not so surprising. I sometimes wonder if she knew about his..." she gave a slight cough, "...proclivities."

Ada was both bemused and intrigued by the change in the old lady's demeanour. Clearly her primness was vulnerable to vanity. "And the women?" she prompted.

"There have been so many of them, but my fondest memories were when I was involved with Saddlers Wells for a short time. Maria Callas and Joan Sutherland - such magnificent artistes. After her death, Miss Callas was labelled a diva in the derogatory sense, but I can tell you from personal experience that she was simply a perfectionist."

"What an amazing life you must have led," said Ada, deliberately putting a stop to the line of conversation. It would not do to exhaust the subject too soon, for there was always the possibility that it may need to be resurrected. "And what about you, Miss Katherine? Were you in an interesting profession?"

From the corner of her eye, Ada saw Elizabeth Wilson stiffen. Indeed, her thin pink neck had risen several inches above her collar, so that she resembled a dyspeptic vulture. If Katherine was aware of her sister's anxiety, she gave no sign as she answered the question.

"I was what we would call a 'lady's companion'. This was not as restrictive as you may think, for it gave me the opportunity to travel extensively. Back then, flying was in its infancy, and ships and railways were the preferred method of transport.

"Unfortunately, the romance of travel is now dead. I well remember the bustling platforms and the porters who seemed capable of small miracles. Half the excitement was the journey itself. Nowadays, you book one day and arrive the next."

As Katherine paused to drink her sherry, Ada felt a foot brush her leg under the table. Her eyes flicked between the sisters. Which of them had done it? Was it simply a case of recrossing the legs, or had it been some sort of signal?

Katherine placed her glass on the table and then addressed Ada. "But, enough about me. What about you? If I had to guess, I'd say you were a retired schoolteacher."

Ada smiled and shook her head. "To use modern terminology, I have been a domestic engineer all my life."

"A noble profession," remarked Elizabeth pompously. "In bygone days, most domestics were trustworthy and reliable."

The smile slipped from Ada's face. She was annoyed at the old lady's superiority. "They still are," she remarked somewhat tartly.

Perhaps sensing that her sister had given offence, Katherine pointed to Ada's wedding ring and said, "I take it you're married?"

Ada used the opening to test the sisters' reactions. She dropped her head, fingered her ring, and mumbled, "A recent widow." She was using body language to create the impression that her grief was still raw, which in truth, it was.

There was no gush of sympathy or overtures of understanding. Instead, the sisters politely averted their eyes. Ada mentally 'shrugged'. Oh well, she thought, it was worth a try.

To break the melancholy silence, she asked Katherine about the brooch pinned to the collar of her blouse. Set in antique gold and fashioned in the shape of a cartouche, it featured a ruby scarab surrounded by white, red, and green stones.

"It was my mother's," she explained, sadness coming into her eyes. "It's practically the only item of hers that I have left. I wear it all the time."

Firmly but not unkindly, Elizabeth said, "That will do, Katherine. You know how upset you get when you become nostalgic. But, speaking of possessions, do not forget to pack yours tonight."

Ada raised an inquiring eyebrow. "Are you leaving the hotel?" she asked, wondering if it had anything to do with the spate of practical jokes. To her surprise, the innocent question provoked a reaction that was far from sedate.

"Leaving?" repeated Elizabeth imperiously. "The only manner in which I will ever leave this hotel is in a pine box!"

"Oh, Elizabeth," cried her sister, "don't say that. I couldn't bear it if anything happened to you."

Katherine produced a handkerchief and dabbed her eyes. Elizabeth however, rather than being sensitive to her sister's feelings, seemed irritated by the filial declaration.

"Oh, do stop twittering. I have no intention of leaving this mortal coil, at least not yet." She turned to Ada. "Please forgive my sister. She is highly-strung and has a tendency to overreact.

"But, to answer your question, Katherine and I are changing rooms. There is a problem with the heating in hers and she is susceptible to cold. Fortunately, my constitution is much more robust."

"Oh, I see," replied Ada, relieved that she was not about to lose a source of information. "Did you speak to Mr Ayres about the heating?"

Once again Elizabeth's reaction was explosive. "Cedric Ayres is an incompetent fool! Even if the roof caved-in, he'd only repair it with one of those cover things."

It took Ada a moment to work out what a 'cover thing' was. "Do you mean a tarpaulin?" she asked, but it seemed the old lady had not finished 'venting her spleen'.

"He has neither taste nor manners, nor will he put his hand in his pocket to spend a little money on improvements."

Ada thought of Florrie's recent bathroom renovation. 'A little money' had been the last thing it had cost. She was about to remark as such when she changed her mind. She was sure the sisters were at their ease with her. Therefore, rather than a

47

frivolous comment, she steered the conversation in another direction.

"You mentioned a Miss Davenport earlier. Who was she?"

It was Katherine who answered, her eagerness betraying that she'd been waiting to voice her earlier interrupted opinion. "Well, it was like this," she began, but got no further.

"May I buy you ladies a drink?" said a male voice. The 'scoundrel' was standing by the table, an empty beer glass in his hand.

Chapter 4. Shock & Surprise.

The reaction of the sisters could not have been more different. Katherine gasped and hunched her shoulders, as if trying to make herself as small as possible. Elizabeth, however, was no shrinking violet. She sat unnaturally still, like a medusa who'd turned herself to stone.

"No, Major Eaton, you may not." Her mouth was little wider than a coin slot, which had the peculiar effect of enhancing her haughtiness. "I was not amused by your crude attempt at humour this morning."

There was a moment of silence in which Ada heard him sigh. Was it exasperation or annoyance she wondered? Clearly this was not the first time the spinster and the Major had locked horns.

"Miss Elizabeth," he said patiently, "I have absolutely no idea what you're talking about. If you have a complaint then I suggest you take it to Mr Ayres – as you usually do."

"I will not bandy words. What do you want?"

"As we don't get too many people of our maturity in the hotel, I thought I would make our new guest welcome in the customary manner." He paused, looked directly at Elizabeth Wilson, and finished on a note of sarcasm. "That's assuming you have no objection."

Their animosity was palpable, and Ada acted quickly to prevent the spinster from uttering a second refusal. "Why, thank you, Major, mine's a whiskey."

Major Eaton went to the bar, returning with a tray of drinks and a bowl of peanuts. He sat between Elizabeth and Ada and raised his glass in salute. "Cheers," he said amiably, and took a drink.

In what Ada considered an act of blatant hypocrisy, the sisters' accepted the drinks but did not return the salutation. Nor did either seem inclined to formally introduce him. If the Major was offended by the snub, he gave no sign as he held out a hand.

"Major Charles Eaton, Army Signal Corps, retired, but everyone calls me Major."

"Mrs Ada Harris, housewife, semi-retired." As they laughed at the old-fashioned formality, Elizabeth Wilson looked away in disgust. Her sister however, almost smiled.

Ada revived an earlier question. "Have you been here long, Major?"

"Let me put it this way, when I first came here, there were still gas masks and tin helmets under the bed." The Major took a swig of beer before asking, "Are you here on holiday, Mrs Harris?"

"Please call me Ada. And the answer is yes and no. I had a slight accident a few weeks ago, and my doctor suggested that I go somewhere nice to recuperate, and so I thought what better place than the seaside."

Elizabeth Wilson, who had been staring sightlessly at the bar, turned her head slightly. In spite of her attitude of indifference, it could not have been clearer that she was listening to every word. Ada decided to employ a little subterfuge of

50

her own, and instead of her hip, she massaged her right shoulder.

Seemingly oblivious to the by-play, the Major continued, "And are you staying long?"

Ada's answer was deliberately non-committal. "Just a few days, but if the weather holds, I might stay a bit longer."

As she took a sip of her whiskey, she noticed that the woman in the garish yellow dress was staring in her direction. Was she looking at her or something behind her? Ada itched to turn around, but instead, she smiled at the woman and inclined her head.

The gesture of civility was not reciprocated. The woman gave her a withering look and snobbishly turned away. Ada seized the opportunity to glance behind her. Nobody was entering the lounge and nothing seemed amiss.

She turned back just as the Major said to Elizabeth, "Now, my dear, please be so kind as to tell me what you were referring to earlier."

The old lady pursed her lips again. "Major Eaton, as you are already acquainted with the facts, I will not gratify your perverseness by recalling them for your pleasure."

His affability disappeared quicker than snow in a desert. "Now, look here! Either explain yourself or apologise for that baseless remark."

In the relative silence of the room, the Major's raised voice had sounded as loud as a foghorn. More than one head turned in his direction. Ada pretended to be interested in a fake anchor suspended from the ceiling. A battle of wills was taking place, and she fervently hoped Katherine would not choose that moment to interrupt.

Seemingly realising they were the focus of attention, Elizabeth Wilson tempered her tone. "My Sunday supplement was not the publication I was expecting. It was replaced with something considerably more distasteful - a pornographic magazine."

Katherine gasped and clutched at her brooch. It was a poignant gesture, as though the utterance of the word 'pornographic' let alone its meaning, would somehow assail her dead mother's ears. But, once again sibling sympathy was in short supply.

"Do not be prudish, Katherine. If the word pornographic is in the dictionary, then it's obviously part of the English language."

"Well...yes...I suppose you're right," she twittered. "But, why didn't you tell me? I suppose it was one of those horrid practical jokes," and so saying, she cast an accusatory glance at the Major.

"Of course it was," replied Elizabeth snappishly. "You are oversensitive as it is, so what would be the point of telling you about it?"

The atmosphere around the table was as thick as treacle. Major Eaton 'thinned' it somewhat when he said, "I can understand your distress, Miss Elizabeth, but I assure you - as I have tried to reassure you before, that I have nothing to do with these jokes. You have my word as a gentleman."

His appeal had little effect. Katherine Wilson stared at the floor as though inspecting the carpet for fleas, while Elizabeth's self-righteous attitude did not waver. Seemingly unconcerned that he was 'persona non grata', Major Eaton shrugged and withdrew a newspaper from his pocket.

"Speaking of words," he said, "I haven't done the crossword today. Would you like to help me complete it?"

Ada was glad of the diversion. In truth, the bickering sisters were becoming annoying. Even so, she had already decided that, somehow, she would separate Katherine from her domineering sister and have a 'little chat'. In the interim, she could do no better than to follow the Major's lead.

"Marvellous," she said. "I love doing crosswords, but I must warn you that I'm not very good at them." Instantly she had a mental picture of Florrie wagging a finger and saying reproachfully, 'Ada Harris - you fibber!'

Thus encouraged, the Major spread the newspaper on the table. After a moment's hesitation in which she seemed to decide whether to be a party pooper or not, Elizabeth Wilson reached into her handbag and withdrew a pair of spectacles.

The lenses were thick and rather scratched, which both enlarged and distorted her green eyes. It reminded Ada of Florrie's comment about looking like a frog. Katherine Wilson was seemingly endowed with 20/20 vision, for she simply leaned forward and read the clues.

With a temporary truce now in effect, Ada & Co began to complete the crossword. On the other side of the room, the impeccably dressed man in his 40's was dictating to his pretty companion, who was furiously scribbling in a notebook.

Two tables across, the fiftyish couple had barely moved. The man still had his nose in a book, and the woman in the garish yellow dress was drumming her fingers on the table. The majority of the patrons were talking quietly, and the barman was busy polishing glasses. Everything appeared perfectly normal, and yet they were being watched.

**

How much longer do I have to wait? Him there - Mr Squeaky-Clean businessman, since when do you play footsies with the hired help? If that's his secretary then I'm a belly dancer. What about Miss Sour Puss? She looks like an overstuffed canary in that dress. I wish I could wring her neck. What about the new one? She keeps rubbing her shoulder. Perhaps I should arrange a little welcome surprise. Nothing too elaborate - at least not yet. As for Miss Prim & Proper and her moronic sister, another push will get them out.

**

The last crossword clue had just been completed when the barman rang a large brass bell. "Ladies and gentlemen, the dining room is now open."

Several people rose at once and headed for the door. The Major folded the newspaper and put it in his pocket. "Is it six o'clock already? May I escort you ladies into dinner? And perhaps, Ada, you would do me the honour of dining with me?"

"Why, thank you, Major," she said graciously, "I accept."

Elizabeth Wilson returned her spectacles to her handbag and stood up. "No, thank you. Katherine and I will sit at our usual table."

Whether by accident or design, she had misconstrued the Major's invitation. He opened his mouth as though to correct the mistake and then seemingly changed his mind. While the iciness between them had not entirely melted, at least there were signs of a thaw.

Meanwhile, Ada was trying not to laugh. The endearment she usually reserved for Florrie, that of 'silly old fool', sprang to her lips, but like the Major, she too thought it prudent to be silent.

***

They exited the cocktail lounge as a group, and upon entering the dining room, split into pairs. The Major and Ada sat by a window that looked directly onto the sea. The sisters headed for a corner with a 'reserved' sign on a table.

Like the foyer, the dining room décor was mismatched. However, there was nothing incongruous about the food, and after an excellent meal of consommé, roast lamb, and Peach Melba, Ada was completely satiated.

In spite of Miss Elizabeth's poor opinion of him, the Major was good company, entertaining his guest with stories of high jinx in his military days. He even made a confession. "I was born and raised on a farm. I was a strapping lad for my age, and instead of being 18 when I enlisted, I was only 16. I remember watching the moon landing on a flickering black & white television in the mess."

"Most people of our generation remember where they were then," she replied. "I once saw a documentary where they tried to prove that the moon landing was a fake."

"Poppycock!" He wiped his mouth on a napkin and stood up. "Please excuse me for a few minutes. I have an urgent letter to send and want to catch the last post."

He left the dining room, leaving Ada to drink her coffee. But the picture of contentment was not quite what it seemed. Bert had stated on the phone a few nights earlier, "The police think that the murder of Alistair Walsh is a robbery gone wrong, but I'm not so sure. Considering the place was packed with tourists, the killer must have been very desperate to take such a risk.

"As for Miss Davenport, it would be easy to dismiss the manner of her death as a bizarre accident. But it also suggests revenge, and given her age, the motive probably lies in her past. I suggest you focus on older people, though of course, they are not exclusive to crime."

Ada studied the other diners. The immaculately dressed 40ish man and the young woman were speaking in hushed whispers, their heads' so close that they almost touched. The 50ish man was still reading a book, and his yellow-clad companion was toying with a fork. The other diners were either chatting, eating, or holding hands. If there was a killer amongst them, he or she was blending in well.

***

The Major returned to the dining room, his cheeks a little flushed as if he'd been hurrying. He was about to order more coffee when Ada stifled a yawn. The Major acted like a gentleman. He summoned a waitress, and rejecting Ada's offer to go 'Dutch', paid the bill.

"Can I interest you in a nightcap?" he asked as they entered the foyer, which even in the wake of the subdued chattering in the dining room, seemed deathly quiet.

"Oh, no, thank you. It's been a long day and I'm very tired."

Major Eaton smiled in understanding. "I see Ayres is not at his post again," he commented, indicating the vacant reception desk. "Strange fellow though friendly enough. Now, would you like me to escort you to your room?"

Ada pressed the button for the lift. "That's very kind of you but I can manage quite well."

"Thank you for a pleasant evening, Ada. I'll see you in the morning for breakfast - goodnight."

Ada made no comment as she entered the lift, and as the doors slowly closed, she saw him walk down the corridor to the cocktail lounge. She also caught a glimpse of Mr Ayres emerging from the door behind the desk, his expression one of perplexity.

***

Ada entered her room and then stopped dead. Everything appeared as she had left it, and yet her instinct screamed that something had changed. And then she smelt a tangy odour of aftershave.

Her immediate thought was that the Major had used the letter as an excuse to covertly visit her room. But, why? For what purpose? Moreover, how had he gained access when the key had been in her handbag all evening?

She shook her head. No, it was too early to judge anyone. There would be plenty of time to form opinions in the coming days. In the meantime, a nice hot bath and a good night's sleep would do her the world of good.

She kicked off her shoes and picked up the suitcase. Next moment, both she and her luggage were on the floor, her shoulder almost wrenched from its socket.

Chapter 5. The Chatty Valet.

It took Ada several moments to recover from the shock. Then, like a commando crawling over a wall, she used the bedspread to pull herself upright. She went into the bathroom and looked at herself in the mirror.

"Ada," she said to her reflection, "you're getting too old for this. Either someone made a good guess or you're being watched."

After drinking a glass of water, she returned to the room and lay the suitcase flat on the floor. She cautiously unzipped the lid. Her clothing had been used to wrap four rectangular objects. She tentatively lifted one out. The object was solid and heavy, and one glance was enough to reveal what it was.

Her shoulder throbbed mercilessly as she unpacked the remaining clothes, which much to her relief were all intact. She returned the now unwrapped objects to the suitcase, closing the lid but not zipping it shut.

She went to the phone beside the bed and dialled reception. She did not know if the man who answered was Mr Ayres or a night porter, and nor did she care. Her gander was up. "This is Mrs Harris in room 26. Is Mr Travis on duty?"

"Yes," he answered, a slight note of suspicion in his voice.

"Please send him to my room," and without further explanation she replaced the receiver.

'If you're the calmest person in the room then you're the only one thinking straight'. This had been one of her husband's many maxims, and to this end, Ada closed her eyes, took deep steadying breaths, and massaged her now genuinely injured shoulder.

Then, more for something to do till the valet arrived, she examined the contents of the nightstand. There was the obligatory bible, a leather bound writing portfolio, and a pamphlet on the hotel.

The front cover showed the hotel on a bright sunny day, but as the portico and marble steps were remarkably clean and white, the picture had obviously been touched up. The inside pages listed amenities, opening hours, and local places of interest, some of which appealed to her.

The back page gave a brief history of the hotel. Built in 1890 for a family of fifteen, the residence passed through various hands until it became a convalescent hospital during World War I. Afterwards, it returned to private ownership, and was eventually purchased in 1945 by William Frederick Ayres, who transformed it into a hotel. He ran it along with his sons until his death in 1967.

Ada was reading the places of interest again when there was a tap on the door. She returned the pamphlet to the drawer and put her slippers on. "Who is it?" she asked through the still closed door. She would not be caught 'napping' a second time.

"Travis."

"Thank you for coming," she said by way of preamble. She quietly locked the door behind him before asking, "Who has a key to my room?"

"Apart from yourself, nobody."

She raised a sceptical eyebrow. "No master key?"

"Yes, but you have the only single key."

Even though Ada was considerably shorter than the valet, she still managed to look him in the eyes as she announced, "Mr Travis, somebody has been in this room and played a practical joke." She went to the suitcase and using her foot, flipped the lid open.

The young man's face turned grey when he saw the four objects. "Oh, my God! I...I...I have absolutely no idea how they got there."

Ada now switched roles. The loveable roly-poly grandma disappeared, replaced by a competent interrogator. "Sit down," she commanded. "I have a few questions to ask."

As Travis stepped over the suitcase and sat in the armchair, Ada recalled another of her late husband's maxims. 'When a person is placed in a compromising situation, then generally speaking, they only have two choices – to do, or not to do'. In other words, either the valet would tell her what she wanted to know, or tell her to go jump.

She judged from the valet's acquiescence and anxiousness that the former would be the case. Therefore, no hard-line tactics would be needed - just a firm hand and where applicable, gentle persuasion.

"Mr Travis," she began, sitting on the bed, "I want to know everything you know about a Miss Davenport, especially in relation to her death. Omit nothing, no matter how insignificant or trivial, even if it's something you did not tell, or forgot to tell, the police."

It crossed her mind that, given she'd only been in the hotel a few hours, he might wonder how she knew the name Miss Davenport. But, the notion seemed not to occur to him for he answered the question immediately.

"Miss Davenport was a long-term resident and spent most of her time knitting in front of the picture window in the cocktail lounge. She loved to watch the ocean. In fact, she became so good at judging the weather, that she could predict up to two days ahead when a storm would hit.

"Approximately three months ago, she retired to her room after playing cards with the Wilson sisters in the lounge, and when she didn't appear at breakfast the next morning, Elizabeth Wilson became concerned and alerted Mr Ayres."

Ada held up a hand to interrupt. "Was Elizabeth's concern based on anything in particular?"

"I don't know, but they were definitely close friends. Perhaps they knew each other years ago."

As he paused to clear his throat, Ada noticed that he was nervously twisting his hands. Moreover, there was a film of sweat on his forehead. "Would you like a drink of water?" she asked.

He nodded and she went into the bathroom, and while rinsing out a glass she gathered her thoughts. She knew she could be overbearing at times, even intimidating - it was part & parcel of her 'second career'. And yet he was edgy after only one question.

Only once had she completed a 'job' very quickly, and that was because the murderer had left his engraved watch at the scene of the crime. Was the valet hiding something, or had he been fond of the old lady and was upset at having to recall her death?

Ada returned with the glass of water. He drank half and then stared at his polished black shoes. So great was his distraction, that there could have been an elephant in the room and he wouldn't have noticed.

"Go on," she gently urged.

"After Miss Elizabeth raised the alarm, Ayres opened the door with the master key and found Miss Davenport...impaled." His eyes began to fill with tears. "The night before had been particularly warm, and someone had put knitting needles on the topside of the ceiling fan. When the fan was turned on, the needles flew like spears and hit her in the chest."

Ada silently counted to 10, thus giving him time for composure. "What happened next?" she asked.

Mr Travis wiped his eyes as he answered, "The police were very thorough, which did surprise me a little given we'd had a murder the day before. Upper Markham is not exactly London or Birmingham, so I imagine the police were stretched to the limit.

"Anyway, I told them everything I knew, and they seemed particularly interested in the fact that, the night before, I saw Miss Elizabeth and Miss Davenport enter the lift together. They were chatting like budgies and Miss Davenport seemed very excited about something."

63

"Did you hear what they said?"

"No. The police interviewed everyone in the hotel, but nobody knew anything. I spoke to an Inspector Butler several times. He said that on the balance of probability, the needles on the ceiling fan was the mode of death as there was no other evidence to contradict it." He paused and then added as an afterthought, "I suppose he was right."

In truth, Ada already knew all the facts, and so far, the valet's statement had been correct. It was the titbits, the impressions and opinions she wanted, and his uncertainty was an opportunity for exploration.

"You sound doubtful. What do you think happened?"

"I don't know," he said slowly. "I mean, it was just so…well, personal. Sorry, I can't quite explain what I mean."

Ada recalled the time when, through remote association, she recovered a stolen document thanks to a little girl and her doll. She now employed the same tactic.

"Put it into terms you can relate too, no matter how silly it sounds."

Mr Travis thought for a moment and then said, "The death of that London solicitor seems opportunistic compared to that of Miss Davenport. The police are convinced her death was a practical joke that went horribly wrong, but I'm not so sure.

"You see it all the time on cop shows. If the victim is known to the killer, that is to say, that they actually know each other, then more often than not, there's a personal element to the manner in which the crime was committed.

"In the case of Miss Davenport, it was the knitting needles. She was rarely seen without her knitting bag, which to me, suggests that her death was not an accident."

Ada was impressed by his deductive reasoning. "That is a very good analogy. I suppose…What is it?"

The valet was looking at her as if he'd just had a revelation of biblical proportion. "I've just realised something. The Major was not in the hotel when she died, therefore he can't be the practical joker."

His frankness and emotional state certainly suggested innocence, and yet Ada was not quite ready to eliminate him from her enquiry. Once before she had dismissed someone too soon and it had almost cost a life. Consequently, she chose her next words with care.

"Not necessarily. There is no way of knowing how long the needles were on the fan before it was turned on."

"I hadn't thought of that," he responded. "I like the Major. It would be horrible if he's guilty."

"You said earlier that Miss Davenport seemed to be excited about something. Was she easily excited? Was she one of those old women who fuss over nothing, or was she someone who just plodded along and smiled at the world?"

Mr Travis smiled for the first time. "Definitely the latter. She was very sweet. I think she was very happy here. Mind you, if something really annoyed her she wouldn't hold back. When someone sprinkled itching powder on the ball of wool she was using, she gave Ayres hell over it."

"When was this?"

"It was just before the summer season started in earnest, so that would make it about four months ago."

The late Mr Harris once said, "The subconscious is a vast yet silent repository of knowledge. The key is to use the right prompt, and sometimes the simplest question can elicit a great result." Though Ada did not consciously associate this pearl of wisdom with her next line of questioning, the result complied with the statement.

"Do you know if Miss Davenport received any letters or phone calls?"

"No. Ayres guards the reception desk as if it was the entrance to Downing Street."

"What about visitors or relatives?"

"None that I know of...oh wait, she once mentioned a cousin, but as I told the police, I don't remember the name."

"Did the police follow it up?"

"I don't know, but as she was a spinster, I doubt it."

Although pleased by the revelation, Ada also felt a pang of disappointment. Without a gender, the cousin might prove as elusive as Lord Lucan. She changed the subject.

"You mentioned the solicitor earlier. I don't suppose you happened to see him?"

"No. We were short staffed that day, and Ayres asked me to work a double shift, hence why I was still here when Miss Elizabeth and Miss Davenport got into the lift." He suddenly paused, looked thoughtful, and then shook his head. "No, it's probably nothing."

Ada leaned forward. "What?" she prompted, her eagerness akin to a dog who'd heard its lead rattle and knew it was time for 'walkies'. "Remember, I did ask you to tell me everything, no matter how trite."

"It's just that the solicitor and Miss Davenport were both found dead on the Sunday morning, and the day before, she was out of the hotel most of the afternoon."

"Was that unusual?"

"A little. She usually went to the haberdashers on Saturday afternoon with Elizabeth Wilson, and on the Saturday in question, instead of returning together in time for tea, Elizabeth Wilson came back alone."

A thought flashed through Ada's mind. It was not common knowledge that, although Alistair Walsh was found on a Sunday morning, the post-mortem revealed he'd died at least 12 hours earlier. Why hadn't Miss Davenport returned to the hotel for tea? Had she met the solicitor? If so, then it opened up a plethora of possibilities.

Once again Ada spoke judiciously. "There are any number of reasons why Miss Davenport delayed her return. But, speaking of the haberdashers, do you know if that's where she bought her wool?"

Mr Travis yawned as he replied, "I think so."

With reluctance, Ada brought the interview to an end. "Well, I'd better not keep you any longer.

67

Thank you for talking to me. I really enjoyed our chat."

"What do you want me to do with those?" he asked, standing up and pointing to the four bricks in the suitcase.

"Hmm…leave them for now, but don't mention it to anyone. I would also be grateful if you didn't repeat anything we've discussed."

"My lips are sealed." He looked at her enquiringly. "Special Branch? MI5?"

"At my age?" Ada laughed. "No, nothing like that. I am writing a book on unusual deaths, and when I heard about Miss Davenport's, I decided to come here and learn what I could." It was not the first time she had used this type of excuse and it probably wouldn't be the last.

The valet walked to the door and was about to open it when she said, "By the way, where's the nearest telephone box?"

He pointed to the phone by the bed. "If you want to make a call, just dial 5 for an outside line."

Ada grinned. "Not if I'm out of the hotel at the time."

His ears flushed pink as he realised his mistake. "There are two within walking distance. Turn right out of the hotel and the first box is on the ocean side near the ice-cream kiosks. The second box is further down on the opposite side in front of the amusement arcade, but don't be surprised if it's broken. Good night."

"Good night."

Ada locked the door behind him and then removed the bricks from her suitcase. Then, retrieving the walking stick from the wardrobe, she used it to push the offending objects under the bed. It was not a matter of retaining evidence, but rather, curiosity as to their fate. When no report of the joke reached the guests, whoever was the culprit might become inquisitive and make a return visit. Whilst the chances of catching him or her in the act were virtually nil, they might be rattled enough to leave a clue, especially in regard to how they were gaining entry.

Ada put on a nightdress and dressing gown and sat in the armchair. There was much to consider, and the valet's recollection of Miss Davenport's death had raised some interesting questions.

To begin with, Elizabeth Wilson was convinced that the Major was the joker, and yet she was too shrewd not to realise that he was not in the hotel when Miss Davenport died. So, why point a finger of blame? Was she being a scandalmonger, or was something else prompting her rancour?

And what of Katherine Wilson. Was she really subservient to her sister or was it a front? Elizabeth had worked in the theatre for years. She had even admitted to being an understudy. Had she taught her sister to act? If so, then either woman could be playing a role.

Ada yawned. Clearly she would have to get closer to the sisters in order to find out more. "But not tonight," she muttered, and without thinking, pushed herself out of the chair.

She yelped in pain. The conversation with the valet had acted like an anaesthetic, and she had completely forgotten about her shoulder. Now however, it throbbed with gusto. At the same time, and as though to keep the shoulder company, her hip began to ache.

She delved into her voluminous handbag and withdrew the medication that 'Doc Mutton-Chops' had prescribed. She took two tablets, set the alarm clock for six, and climbed into bed. Lying in the dark, she tried to listen to the waves lapping the shore but was soon sound asleep. She did not hear the snigger as someone walked past her door.

***

I bet she'll be sore in the morning. Oh, for Christ's sake, why is everything taking so long? Perhaps I should speed things up. Nothing too drastic. The last thing I want is the police sniffing around again. But, who to choose? Ah, yes, Miss Sour Puss. She won't look so glamorous when I've finished with her.

Chapter 6. Phone Calls.

By 6.30 the next morning, Ada was out of the hotel and walking along the foreshore. The sun was peeking through billowy clouds, and a light breeze was blowing off the ocean. It promised to be a beautiful day.

Apart from a smattering of fishermen and dog-walkers, whose exuberance so early in the morning was an offence to the still groggy eyed, there were very few people in sight. Nevertheless, upon reaching the phone box near the ice-cream kiosks, Ada glanced over her shoulder to ensure there was nobody behind her.

She entered the box and lifted the receiver. The number she dialled was so secret that not only were coins unnecessary, but it would never be listed in a telephone directory. It was answered on the third ring, but instead of the expected answering machine, a real voice spoke.

"Hello." The man sounded obscenely alert for such an early hour.

"Morning, Bert, its Ada…yes, everything's fine…bit dingy but the food's good." At any other time, she would have enjoyed a 'chinwag' with her boss, but not today. If she was indeed being watched, then she did not want to be out of the hotel at such an early hour longer than necessary. "Bert, I need you to check something for me, got a pen?"

On the surface, Albert Eagles or Bert to his closest associates, was a pleasant man who enjoyed playing cards and collecting unusual paperweights. He was in his early 60's, always neatly groomed, and could have passed for an accountant or a dentist.

But behind the amiable persona was a man of incredible power. Known colloquially as 'the trouble-shooter, he had access to almost every law enforcement database in the world. From a blood group to a shoe size, there was very little he couldn't find out.

His department was not a spy agency but a solver of awkward problems. Only the highest echelon of government knew it existed, and even fewer knew where its office was located.

Below a famous street in London, a vault was crammed with so many compromising reports and seized gadgetry, that had an author of espionage stories been given access, they would have thought all their birthdays had come at once.

Ada had known Bert for 15 years, and his predecessor - who just happened to be his father, for over 30. She could obtain all manner of information, the relevance of which was always included in a written report at the end of a 'job'.

Ada spoke rapidly and then hung up the phone. There was one more piece of information she wanted checked, but as it was a product of curiosity rather than probative value, she was reluctant to go through official channels. She vacillated for a moment and then lifted the receiver again. This time, the phone almost rang out before it was answered.

"Who is it?" demanded a grumpy voice. "You'd better have a good reason for waking me up at this time of the morning."

"Oh, shut up you silly old fool, it's me."

Florrie sat bolt upright, all trace of sleepiness gone. "Ada? What's wrong? Why are you ringing me so early?"

"No particular reason. It's a beautiful morning here in Upper Markham."

"You rang to give me a weather report? Ada, that's not funny." Bedsprings creaked down the line as Florrie shifted position. "Are you enjoying your holiday? What's the hotel like?"

"Fine so far. The food is surprisingly good and the hotel is just as the advert stated, quiet and comfortable, though it's a bit run down. How are things back there?"

"Apart from the fact that Mr Simpkins left me another present last night, everything's fine."

Ada chuckled as she said, "I think it's time he went home."

This was a long-standing joke. Mr Simpkins was a ginger tom who had wandered into Florrie's home ten years earlier and taken up residence. Since then, in return for letting him scratch the furniture and sleep anywhere he liked, he would often show his appreciation by leaving a dead mouse - usually decapitated, on the kitchen floor.

When the rodent was tossed into the bin, the cat would look at Florrie as though to say, 'well, if that's what you think of my present, I'll pack my toys and leave', but he never did.

Conscious of the passing minutes, Ada changed the subject. "Listen, Florrie, I don't have much time. The line will drop out and I don't have any more change. I want you to do something for me."

"Let me get a pen." The bedsprings creaked again. "Okay, go ahead."

"I want you to go to the Public Records Office and check…" Ada glanced at her watch as she talked. She had now been out of the hotel nearly half an hour. In addition, not only was the sun heating the phone box, but her stomach was grumbling loudly.

"Got that?" she finished.

"Yes, but why do you want to know?"

Ada felt a pang of guilt. She had never been comfortable lying to her friend. "It's to do with a competition at the hotel. Tell you about it when I come home."

On the other end of the phone, Florrie looked at her notes. She had kept her suspicions to herself for years, and now by way of a lame excuse - and she was sure that's what it was, Ada was involving her in…whatever it was she was involved in.

Not knowing exactly what that 'something' was, Florrie knew she was in no position to confront her friend. Even so, there was nothing wrong with dropping a hint.

"Has this anything to do with your innumerable, not to mention elusive, relatives?"

The silence across the miles of coaxial cable was deafening. Ada's sudden impersonation of a ventriloquist's doll - opening and closing its mouth without making a sound, would have gone down a treat on a vaudevillian stage.

There were not too many times in her long, arguably adventurous life when she had not known what to say, but Florrie's question and its underlying ramifications had literally left Ada speechless. And yet this was such a pivotal moment in their enduring friendship, that it was vital she say something plausible before the line dropped out.

Ada felt sweat between her shoulders as she answered, "The truth? Absolutely nothing. I have stumbled across something rather odd and curiosity has got the better of me."

There was no response. Clearly Florrie was unconvinced. Ephectic thought Ada, which gave her an idea. She delved into her repertoire of unusual words and produced one of the more humorous.

"Porcipophagic."

"Eh?" responded Florrie nasally. "What does that mean?"

"Pig eating. I'm about to eat a big breakfast with lots of bacon. Talk to you later."

But Florrie had not quite finished. Boyd by the fact that Ada had not altogether fobbed her off, she took a deep breath and in her most serious voice, made a remark that was both a hint and genuine concern.

"Please be careful, Ada. I don't want you coming home in an ambulance again. I'll be in touch – ta ta."

***

Walking back to the hotel, Ada unfastened her coat and let the breeze cool her down. It had been 'hot' in the phone box in many respects. When Florrie had something on her mind, she usually voiced it with the subtlety of a Sherman tank. Nor

75

did she give two hoots for 'political correctness'. She was not being rude or inconsiderate, nor was she deliberately being offensive. It was simply that if she wanted to know something, she would ask. Therefore, to drop hints instead of speaking plainly was contrary to her nature.

'There's no fool like an old fool', she thought. Was she the one being foolish, continuing to believe that after all these years, Florrie was in ignorance of her, Ada's, 'second' career? Perhaps it was time to come clean.

She was still considering the question when she entered the hotel. Mr Ayres was fiddling with some papers behind the reception desk. "Ah, good morning, Mrs Harris. Been for a morning constitutional?"

"Good morning, Mr Ayres. Yes, I thought I would blow the cobwebs away."

He lowered his voice and said conspiratorially, "As the saying goes, the early bird gets the worm, so if you want the choicest selection, I suggest you have breakfast now before the other guests arrive."

All this was said with a sugary smile that was as fake as a cheap toupee. Ada managed a smile of gratitude and entered the dining room. The first person she saw was the Major. He was sitting at the same table they'd occupied the previous evening, and the tableaux he presented was a still-life photographers dream.

Completely lost in thought, he had a teacup poised halfway to his lips, but whether he was picking it up or putting it down was open to interpretation. So contemplative was his expression, that Ada almost felt guilty about disturbing him.

"Good morning, Major," she greeted, removing her hat and coat.

Startled out of his reverie, the Major jerked the cup. Drops of tea spilt over the rim and stained the stark white tablecloth. "Oh, good morning, Ada." He stood up and pulled out a chair for her. "I know I said last night that I'd meet you for breakfast but I don't think we set a time, and so I came down early so as not to miss you."

"You didn't have to do that," she said with a smile, wondering if he'd seen her returning from the phone box.

"Think nothing of it, dear lady. I hope you're hungry. Breakfast is served buffet style and it's usually pretty good."

"Yes, so Mr Ayres has just informed me." She stood up. "Excuse me while I inspect the bill of fare."

She went across and looked at the contents of numerous warming trays. The bacon was overdone for her liking, and the scrambled eggs appeared a little runny. Nevertheless, she put some on a plate and added two sausages.

Returning to the table, she had just started to eat when she was greeted a third time. "Good morning, Ada," said Elizabeth Wilson. Katherine also stood by the table, her eyes red-rimmed as though she'd been crying.

Ada wiped her mouth on a napkin and returned the greeting, noting that the salutation did not extend to the Major, who seemed completely unperturbed by the lack of civility.

"If you have no plans this morning," Elizabeth went on, "my sister and I intend revisiting the past. Would you care to join us?"

Ada blinked confusedly. "I beg your pardon?"

"What my sister means," twittered Katherine, "is that we're going to the old part of town before it disappears forever. Admittedly there's not much to see but it's a pleasant walk."

Ada recalled what the taxi driver had said - 'If you get the chance, visit the pier. The whole area's being flattened'. Though she had little interest in architecture, the opportunity to spend time with the sisters away from the hotel was too good to miss.

"Thank you. I'd like that very much."

"Be in the foyer at 9 o'clock," said Elizabeth brusquely. It sounded more like a command than an invitation, and Ada was tempted to throw her a salute.

Elizabeth finally looked at the Major, or more accurately, his plate of food. To judge from her expression, had there been a shaker of cyanide laced salt to hand, she would have sprinkled it over his eggs.

"Enjoy your breakfast, Ada," she added in a pitying tone, and with her sister following like a puppy, they went to their table in the corner.

The Major waited until they were out of earshot before saying, "I had intended to show you around the town myself. There is a wonderful fish & chip shop at the other end of the foreshore. It boasts that the fish is so fresh that it still has the hook in its mouth."

Although he'd put a brave face on it, the note of bitterness in his voice betrayed his annoyance at being thwarted by his nemesis. Ada felt a little like the 'meat in the sandwich'. So far, the Major had been kind and courteous, and yet Elizabeth seemed determined to belittle him at every opportunity.

Ada smiled in appreciation. "It sounds heavenly. Perhaps tomorrow for lunch?"

The Major seemed mollified. "As the Americans say, it's a date."

Chapter 7. Down Memory Lane.

Ada met the sisters at precisely nine o'clock. They were wearing the same ensembles as yesterday - Elizabeth in her pseudo Mary Poppins outfit, and Katherine in her 'farmer's wife' garb.

Led by Elizabeth, as they exited the hotel and turned right, Ada realised that, even though Mr Ayres had been at the reception desk, they had not left their keys behind.

Shrugging, she followed the sisters passed a long line of shops, houses, and non-descript buildings. Some of the shops were open, no doubt hoping to cash-in on the last of the tourist trade, but the majority were either closed or empty.

The houses had a similar appearance, in that some still had signs of life – a bicycle or pair of boots near the front door, but it was clear from the accumulated detritus, the overgrown gardens, and the boarded-up windows, that many were unoccupied.

There was no sign of neglect or desertion at the amusement arcade. Catchy music blasted the street, and the exterior pulsated with thousands of coloured lights. The psychedelic montage was enough to give the highly-strung or anyone over the age of 40 a headache.

The road ahead curved to the right, and upon clearing the apex, Ada saw a dilapidated pier. Large sections of the railing were missing, and all the pylons, some of which were leaning at a 45-degree angle, were rotten and encrusted with barnacles. One fierce storm and the structure would collapse.

The right side of the pavement was lined with the same yellow bollards that Ada had seen yesterday. She had not been able to judge their size through the taxi window, but now that she was closer and stationary, she saw that it would take a fireman's ladder to reach the top.

And yet undaunted by the equivalent of climbing a vertical mountain - or perhaps it was just pig-headedness, the graffiti artists had left their marks, most of which were incomprehensible. The lower tags were partially obscured by posters and notices, though whether this was deliberate or sheer opportunism was unclear.

Without warning and with surprising agility, Elizabeth Wilson quickened her pace. Ada and Katherine literally had to run to keep up. When Elizabeth finally stopped, not only was she directly opposite the pier, but there were tears in her eyes.

"My God, Katherine, look at the state of it! How could they do this?"

"Was it a popular spot?" asked Ada, trying not to wince. The run might have only been a hundred feet or so, but to her tender hip it had felt like a marathon.

Elizabeth, whose only sign of exertion were bright pink spots on her cheeks, pointed to the footpath. "There used to be a lovely teashop right here. The past is being dismantled stone-by-stone and nobody gives a damn."

"You can't stop progress," said Ada. "Like the march of time, it cannot be held back."

"Spare me the platitudes. The price of progress is consumerism, materialism, and celebrity worship. Modern society has corrupted all that is decent and good."

"I take it this area holds fond memories for you?"

"For both of us," said Katherine quietly.

Another maxim of the late Mr Harris was that 'nostalgia could expose more than the past'. Ada thought of this as she looked from one sister to the other. Each in their own way was experiencing deep emotion, and she had only a moment to decide whom to manipulate.

"Will you describe it for me, Miss Elizabeth?"

"Civility, charm, and propriety. Women rarely went out without a hat and gloves, and men were polite and chivalrous."

This was not quite what Ada had meant. Nevertheless, it added to the picture. "And the tearoom?" she prompted.

"The waitresses wore black dresses and starched white caps, and food was served on paper doilies. I once suggested this to Mr Ayres but he laughed in my face. Katherine, what was its name?"

"The tearoom? Um…it changed names several times, but I think the last one was 'The China House'."

"Nonsense! The China House is probably somewhere you visited on your travels. Really, Katherine, your memory is getting worse every day. I have the name Parkers in mind."

Katherine lowered her eyes as she responded, "Oh, yes. You're right as usual."

There was a pause, and once again Ada was aware of underlying tension. But, she was on a roll, and she was not about to let anything stop it. She pointed to the dilapidated pier and asked, "Was it the kind that had shops?"

It was Elizabeth who responded, and just as she had done earlier, she spoke in a sentimental voice. "Yes, but they were booths or kiosks rather than actual shops. I remember walking along the pier when I was about five or six. Shortages were still in effect, and yet people were determined to make the best of things. To use a vulgarism, they were sticking two fingers up at Germany."

"Unfortunately," said Ada, "from what I've been told, the post-war optimism had an ugly side. Shysters and profiteers could lay their hands on just about anything, especially from the Americans. Yet despite the inflated prices and questionable quality of goods, my mother said it was a happy time."

"Greed in any era always brings out the worst in people," commented Elizabeth.

"Oh, no," said Katherine timidly, seemingly reluctant to contradict her sister. "What Ada means is that because of shortages and the effects of war, families became much closer and materialism did not have the same value as before. As you just said, people made the best of things."

Until then, Katherine had appeared to be something of a lemming, meekly following and conceding to her sister without question. Now however, she seemed capable of expressing an intelligent opinion, and Ada was both surprised and impressed.

"Very well put. That is exactly what I meant. People were tired of the death and destruction, and all they wanted was a return to normality and to rebuild their shattered lives."

Ada thought her remark reasonable and inoffensive. She was startled by the vehemence of Elizabeth's response. "That is an extremely naive statement to make. Not everyone was fortunate to be in such a position. The widows, the fatherless children, the displaced. Millions of people suffered because of the machinations of one man. It is men who start wars, it is men who ruin women, and yet men are never held accountable."

The spinster could have been a pin-up girl for feminism. She had stated the literal truth, and Ada could not think of a reasonable counter argument. To prevent a debate on the inadequacies of men and the methods by which retribution could be extracted, she changed tack.

"What are they building here?"

Elizabeth sniffed disdainfully. "So-called luxury apartments the size of shoe boxes with vulgar price tags."

"Elizabeth," said her sister, "do you remember the old souvenir shop? It used to sell postcards and buckets & spades. We always dragged father there the first chance we got."

"Are you going senile? It wasn't father, it was mother."

Katherine could not have looked more crest-fallen, and once again Ada felt like the 'meat in the sandwich', which gave her an idea. "I don't know about you, but I could do with a cup of tea. Is there somewhere nearby where we could get one?"

"There is a sort of cafe behind the arcade," replied Elizabeth, but without much enthusiasm. "I would not insult finer establishments by calling it a restaurant. Even deeming it a tearoom is stretching the point."

***

They made the journey in silence, and upon entering the café, Ada did see the spinster's point. It was as far removed from a genteel tearoom as an abattoir. There were no silver teapots, paper doilies, or dainty cakes. Instead, it was a shrine to modernity, the offerings being computer screens, unappetising packaged sandwiches, and an industrial-sized urn.

A scruffy man in his early 60's, whose attitude conveyed that he would rather be at home watching the telly, took their order, and when the three cups of tea arrived, Elizabeth looked at the murky liquid and scowled.

"A teabag," she said in disgust. "Nobody uses real tea nowadays." She glared at the white plastic spoon as if daring it to jump up and do a twisted piked somersault into her cup.

Her sister did not seem perturbed by the lack of refinement. This puzzled Ada for a moment, and then she remembered that Katherine had travelled extensively, and had probably taken refreshment in the most unlikely of places.

Ada saw an opportunity to do a little more 'digging, reasoning that, when it came to personal experience, even the dim witted could be prompted into recollection.

"You said last night that you'd been a lady's companion. You must have had some interesting employers."

"Oh, my word, yes. My first lady was a vicar's daughter, who wanted to see something of the world before settling down. Her father gave his permission, but only on the condition she was accompanied by a 'respectable companion', and through a mutual acquaintance I obtained the post.

"We travelled through France, Holland, Belgium, and Germany, and though it was exciting it was also sobering. Each country still bore the scars of Hitler's maniacal regime. I spoke to many people who had survived the war, and they all more or less said the same thing, that even when the war ended, they were frightened.

"Take a girl of 13 for example. Did she go to school or was she sent to work? Would her education be of benefit or were her wages more important? Even a task such as growing vegetables was regarded with uncertainty. Were the storm troopers going to return and wreak havoc?

"It is a testament to courage and determination that, like a phoenix rising from the ashes, Europe eventually got back on its feet. Thanks to my travels, I was able to observe the progress first-hand.

"Unfortunately, today's generation think the war ended and that was that. They have no conception of the residual effect, especially the damage to society as a whole."

At this, Elizabeth drew in a short sharp breath, ready to interrupt. But once again Ada was having none of it. She did not want the domineering spinster to interrupt the conversation, which no doubt would lead to another lecture on the inadequacies of men. Katherine Wilson had the floor, and what's more, she was giving an interesting speech.

Ada quickly asked, "Were all your ladies strait-laced?"

"Oh, my goodness, no. My last trip to Europe was about three years ago and involved the most eccentric of my ladies. Her full name was Charlotte Annabelle Imogene Roberta Ophelia, which if you take the first letter of each name spells Cairo. Both she and her father were passionate about ancient Egypt, but in my opinion, he couldn't tell the difference between a temple and a templar.

"She had another passion – Pekinese dogs. No matter where we went, those yapping terrors came with us, and of course, they could never do anything wrong."

"Even little 'accidents'?"

"Especially those," replied Katherine with a girlish titter. "It was always somebody else's fault. Either myself or the butler had not opened the door in time."

Ada laughed. "Oh, how precious. You should write a book about your experiences. I would certainly read it, wouldn't you, Miss Elizabeth?"

There was no reply. Elizabeth was sitting rigid in her chair, her down turned mouth conveying abject disapproval. She looked like the bride's mother just before a shotgun wedding.

Drinking the now luke-warm tea, Ada speculated whether jealousy was the source of the sisters' tension. Did Elizabeth resent being stuck behind a stage while her sister had explored the world? If so, then it was a poor reason for treating a sibling as a virtual non-entity.

Before Ada could ask another question, Elizabeth stood up and said, "Speaking of journeys, we should consider our own. We do not want to be late for luncheon."

Katherine looked disappointed. Clearly she had been enjoying herself. She stood up and twittered an acquiescence. She had returned to her old subservient self. The globetrotting old lady had proved too intelligent to be constantly cow towing to her sister, and yet it seemed defiance was not in Katherine's nature.

***

The return pace was anything but casual, and by the time Ada entered the hotel, she was in desperate need of a good cup of tea. The dining room was virtually empty, and after a quick lunch, Ada went to her room.

She removed her hat and coat and then used the walking stick to 'feel' under the bed. A dull 'clunk' told her that the bricks were still there. Satisfied, she withdrew a book from her suitcase, replaced her shoes with slippers, and lay on the bed.

But this was not as innocent as it seemed. Apart from the Wilson sisters, no one of consequence had seen her enter the hotel, and as she knew from bitter experience, there was nothing more frustrating for a secret observer than to lose sight of their quarry. Therefore, it was possible that someone might enter her room when they thought it empty.

Absolutely nothing happened, and by 5 o'clock, Ada was sitting with the sisters in the cocktail lounge. Elizabeth did the honours, and Ada opted for white wine. She was just contemplating how to raise the subject of Miss Davenport when the Major entered.

He did not hesitate to join them, and their activities were a repeat of the previous evening - drinks and the crossword puzzle. Ada rubbed her shoulder several times. At one point, she had a mental image of the muscles and sinews being stretched like rubber bands. She considered visiting a local doctor and then dismissed it. What could he tell her that she didn't already know?

Once again the barman sounded the dinner bell. Ada and the Major sat at the same table in front of the window, and this time he did not disappear during the meal.

'So', thought Ada as she sipped coffee, "if there are more surprises in my suitcase, he cannot be the culprit'. However, this did not automatically grant him immunity, and she was not quite ready to eliminate him as a suspect.

"Did you enjoy your outing?" he asked.

"Yes," she answered, but without expansion.

"I suppose the old harridan spent the morning casting dispersions on my character."

Ada eyed him speculatively and wondered if he was 'fishing'. "Actually, Major, she never mentioned you."

"Really? You surprise me. Perhaps the truth is finally getting through to the old girl." He rubbed his hands and said cheerfully, "Well, you have the other end of the foreshore to look forward to tomorrow."

Ada smiled as she said, "And lovely fish & chips."

Chapter 8. Fish & Chips.

The following morning, Ada met the Major at the reception desk just before nine o'clock. Mr Ayres was at the rear counter and appeared to be tallying accounts. His back was turned, and as the seconds ticked past, Ada had the distinct impression that they were being ignored.

She cleared her throat and said, "Mr Ayres, the Major and I are going out. Here are our keys." There was no response. "Mr Ayres?" she prompted in a louder voice.

"I heard you the first time," he responded gruffly. "Leave your keys on the desk. Have a nice day," he added, though with less sincerity than a cactus.

Exiting the hotel, Ada and the Major turned left and headed in the direction of the railway station. "Cheeky sod," she said. "He did that deliberately."

"He's a strange fellow," responded the Major. "His moods swing like a monkey through the trees."

Ada was tempted to say, 'so do Miss Elizabeth's', but then thought better of it. If there was something 'funny' going on between the alleged combatants, then it would be prudent to appear neutral. She therefore remained silent and focused on the scenery.

Rather than dismal and deserted, this end of the foreshore was vibrant and active, and even though it was early in the week, visitors crowded the pavement. The ritual floppy or straw hat, sunglasses, and a liberal coating of sun tan oil were all in evidence, and Ada admired their optimism, for although the sky was a gorgeous duck-egg blue, the heat from the sun at such an early hour was not particularly strong.

The Major guided her to shops he thought would be of interest. These included an art gallery - whose paintings were predominantly seascapes, a bookstore - where murder and piracy on the high seas seemed to be the dominant theme, and an antiques shop, whose prices were outrageously inflated.

Ada took advantage of his local knowledge to obtain directions. "I forgot to pack a sewing kit and a button has come off a dress. I heard someone mention a haberdashery. Do you know where it is?"

The Major pointed to a side street. "I believe it's up there. Do you want to go there now?"

"Might as well while we're passing."

***

The Major waited outside while Ada entered the shop. She perused the shelves and purchased several lace handkerchiefs, two sets of linen pillowcases, and a set of knitting needles. She thanked the middle-aged woman behind the counter and then checked her watch. It was nearly twelve o'clock. Time for the fish & chips.

She re-joined the Major, and as they strolled towards the promised marine nirvana, he asked, "How's the shoulder today? I hope the injury isn't serious."

Ada donned a mask of polite surprise. "Not at all. I took a tumble down some steps. How did you know I'd hurt my shoulder?"

"You rubbed it several times last night."

"You are very observant."

The Major shrugged. "Not really. As I told you on Sunday night, I was in the Signal Corps, and some army habits are hard to break."

Ada saw no harm in telling a true story of her own. "I know what you mean. My father was in the army and was shot in France. Of course, I wasn't born then, but my mother told me that when he returned to England for treatment, he became a stickler for having his tea at exactly 5.40. Unfortunately, they were never able to safely remove the bullet and eventually it killed him."

"My father died when I was four, and I was packed off to an aunt so that my mother could grieve. I don't remember much about it, but I do know that I was very angry."

"Why?"

"Well, with the benefit of hindsight, I suppose it was because my feelings were ignored. Nobody except Aunt Elspeth seem to recognise that I was hurting too. I missed her terribly when she and her daughter suddenly emigrated to Australia. Ah, here we are."

They had arrived at the fish & chip shop, and the Major ushered her to an outside table. "Fancy the lot?" he asked, his eyes shining in gleeful anticipation.

"Of course," she replied enthusiastically.

***

Major Eaton returned with two cardboard trays. "Got you a pickled onion too," he said as he sat at the table, "but I wasn't sure about the welks so I didn't get you any."

Ada stared hungrily at her lunch. "Welks? Oh, they can wait until later," and cutting into the golden batter, she thought of how Miss Elizabeth would have disapproved of the plastic knife and fork.

The fish was delicious, and as Ada savoured every mouthful, the hot food, coupled with the heat of the midday sun, caused her to sweat. She wriggled out of her coat and swivelled around to hang it on the back of her chair. Nothing could have prevented her cry of pain.

The Major looked up sharply. "Are you alright?" he asked in alarm.

Ada vigorously rubbed her shoulder. "Oh, yes, I just turned too quickly. I keep forgetting that I'm not as young as I used to be." Under the table however, her hip was dancing a rumba.

As Ada continued to eat, she began to ponder the situation. Concrete facts were proving as scarce as hen's teeth, but one coincidence had been firmly established, namely, that both the Major and the Wilson sisters were long time visitors to the hotel. This, she decided, required further probing, and there was no time like the present.

"I think you said the other evening that you've been coming here a long time. Have you always stayed at the Seabridge?"

"Yes. Regrettably, it's one of the last hamlet style hotels that cater for long-term residents. Somebody told me that it saw some hush-hush wartime service, and that the military moved in for a while.

"Anyway, I lived in London when I retired from the army, and even though I worked in the city, I would usually come here for my holidays. Call me sentimental, but there's something about the place that keeps drawing me back."

"And what did you do in the city?"

"I worked in a bank. I have always had an aptitude for numbers, but my brainpower - such as it is, was no match for a computer, and eventually I was made redundant.

"I plodded around for a while and made a living, but it seemed to me that I was only marking time, and so I decided to move here. I only intended to stay at the hotel until I found permanent quarters, but somehow I never got round to it.

"I do get the occasional attack of itchy feet, such as when I went travelling around Scotland a few months ago, but now that I'm practically in my dotage, buying a house or flat here seems pointless. For better or worse, the old Seabridge is my home."

It occurred to Ada that, apart from a childhood story that may or may not be true, he had not divulged any private details. She therefore raised a subject that, on the surface at least, was perfectly natural.

"Any family?" she asked simply.

The pause before he answered was fleeting but discernible. "I never married. What about you?

What is the Ada Harris story? I know you're married because you're wearing a wedding ring."

Ada silently cursed. She had not expected him to quickly turn the spotlight on her. Another maxim of the late Mr Harris was, 'A really good lie is a mixture of fact and fiction, and what's more, you'll usually get away with it'. Ada applied it to her answer – liberally.

"Compared to you, very mundane. I have worked in an office most of my life. I lost my husband a few years ago, and now my grandchildren take up most of my time."

"How many do you have?"

As with the Wilson sisters on Sunday evening, Ada created a melancholy atmosphere. She lowered her eyes and said wistfully, "Three - all in New Zealand. I have lots of photographs of course, but it's not the same as hugging them."

If the Major had lied about his marital status, he would have recognised the familial bond and the pain of separation. In all probability he would have made overtures of sympathy and said something uplifting like, "New Zealand is only a plane ride away." But his response was the same as the sisters - a respectful silence.

Ada sat back in her chair, uncertain how to proceed. He had certainly hesitated when she'd mentioned his family, and yet to pursue the subject was likely to rouse suspicion. Perhaps she was being overly cautious. Perhaps he was exactly what he appeared to be - a lonely old man living out his days in peace.

No sooner had she thought this when instinct, metaphorically speaking, slapped her across the face and told her to wake up. If his entire story was a yarn then she'd almost fallen for it.

She watched the seagulls circling the table. There was a scrap of cold chip in the corner of the cardboard tray. She threw the chip on the ground, and like fighter pilots, the birds dived on the morsel of food. It gave her an idea. It was a long shot but it was worth a try.

"You said the other night that you managed to join the army when you were only sixteen. Did you do any overseas tours?"

Once again he hesitated before answering. "Unfortunately, I can't tell you. I'm still bound by certain sections of the Official Secrets Act." He suddenly stood up and waved his arms like a windmill. "Here! Yes - you! Come over here!"

Chapter 9. Mixed Messages.

For a moment, Ada thought the Major had suddenly gone mad. And then an old style pony and trap stopped near their table. The Major offered her his arm. "I'm too full to walk back to the hotel," he explained.

Ada smiled in appreciation and not just because the trap was a quaint method of transport. The pain in her hip had barely eased, and she also was reluctant to make the long walk back. She took the offered arm, gritted her teeth, and manoeuvred herself into the trap.

The Major addressed the driver. "The Seabridge Hotel if you please, and don't hurry."

The driver saluted and set the horse at walking pace. Ada waited a few minutes for the Major to relax, then, like a novice fisherman hoping for a big catch, she cast a line. "I understand there was a recent tragedy at the hotel."

Major Eaton, who had been gazing at the sea, turned to face her, and for the briefest of moments his eyes narrowed. "So, you've heard about our crime wave."

"Yes. I remember hearing about the London solicitor on the telly some time ago. I had forgotten about it until my taxi driver on Sunday reminded me of it. It does make you wonder why the solicitor was here in the first place. It really annoys me when the media make these types of announcements and then don't provide a follow-up, or if they do, you miss it."

The Major grunted. "I don't pay much attention to the news. I mainly read the newspaper for the sporting pages."

"And the crossword puzzle," put in Ada.

"True. How did you hear about Miss Davenport's death? Was that also on the telly?"

"I don't know. I heard about it from the Wilson sisters. It was one of the first things they told me. Apparently, they knew her. Did you?"

"I never saw her. She died when I was in Scotland, but from what I understand, she had a fatal accident with some knitting needles." He shuddered. "Nasty business."

"Yes, that's more or less what the sisters told me." Ada decided to cast the line a little further. "Pardon my nosiness, Major, but I couldn't help noticing that your friendship with the sisters seems…well, strained. I hope that after all these years you haven't had a falling out."

"Friendship!" The Major was so outraged that Ada thought he would have a fit. "What friendship? I only met them about five or six months ago. I have always tried to be polite and courteous to them, but they think I'm some sort of ogre."

Ada inwardly smiled. The 'fish' was on the hook. All she had to do was reel him in. "Oh, sorry, Major. I assumed that as you and the sisters have been staying at the hotel for years, you knew each other." She silently counted to five and then asked, "Why do you think they don't like you?"

He shrugged. "No idea."

Ada tried not to smile. The 'fish' was in the pot. "I think I know, but I will only tell you if you promise not to repeat it."

The Major made the Boy Scout's salute. "Promise."

"The sisters think you're the practical joker."

He looked at her in astonishment, and Ada expected him to start proclaiming his innocence. Instead, he threw back his head and roared with laughter. Several people on the footpath looked around to see where the noise was coming from.

The Major produced a handkerchief and wiped his streaming eyes. "Oh, Ada, you've made my day. No, I take that back, you've made my year. So that's what's wrong with the old biddies.

"Well, unless I'm a brilliant physicist who can manipulate time and space so that I can be in two places at once, then I must plead innocent. Just after I returned from Scotland, someone put pepper in my toothpaste. I spoke to Ayres about it, and he said the jokes had been happening for weeks.

"In fact, he thinks the sisters are responsible. I can't see it myself. They might be batty and stuck in the past but at least their primness is genuine. I mean, can you honestly imagine them killing someone by accident?"

"Not really," she answered truthfully.

"Neither can I, but..." His voice suddenly trailed away, his eyes glazed and blank. Clearly something had just occurred to him.

Ada felt a tingle of excitement as she prompted, "What is it?"

The Major frowned and looked rather confused, and Ada deduced from his expression that, like Mr Travis, he too was having difficulty putting thoughts into words. Finally, he said, "It's just that someone told me, or perhaps I overheard it somewhere, that after her death, Miss Davenport's knitting bag could not be found."

Ada also frowned. "I'm sorry, Major, but I don't understand."

"Because she never went anywhere without it and she was killed with her own needles."

Ada wished she could take notes. Nevertheless, she pushed on in order not to lose momentum. "Why are the police so certain they were her needles? After all, anyone can buy them. I purchased a set myself at that haberdashery this morning."

"I don't know. Fingerprints I suppose." He half-turned in his seat and looked at her earnestly. "Ada, may I confide in you?"

"Of course."

"Well, what if her death wasn't an accident?"

Ada stiffened. 'He's cottoned on', she thought. She had to deflect him. The last thing she needed was him running around asking awkward questions. "Major," she said in a pitying tone, "why would anyone want to murder a little old lady? From what you've told me, the police investigated the matter and are satisfied that her death was an accident."

He gave her a wan smile. "I suppose you're right," and turning his head, gazed at the ocean again.

Clearly as far as he was concerned, the subject was closed. Ada, however, was far from finished. She sat back in the trap and began to think.

***

Ada was still ruminating when the trap came to a stop. "Are we here already?" she said in surprise. To cover the fact that she had paid little attention to the journey, she quickly added, "It seemed much longer when we were walking."

"It usually does," said the Major. "What seems like miles by foot is probably only a few hundred yards."

After paying the driver, the Major helped Ada out of the trap. Her throbbing hip was now a dull ache, but even so, she moved cautiously.

"I don't know about you," he said as they entered the hotel, "but I could murder a drink." He let out an embarrassed cough. "Sorry. Perhaps under the circumstances that was a bad choice of word."

Ada was only half-listening, her attention having been caught by something interesting. Mr Ayres was standing behind the reception desk, a slip of paper in his hand. His stiff upright manner, his slightly bulging eyes, and his frown of concentration, indicated that he was deeply troubled.

He looked up, saw Ada and the Major approaching, and dropped the slip of paper. "Ah, hello," he greeted, his attitude changing in a nanosecond. "You have some messages, Mrs Harris."

He turned away and retrieved her key, two slips of paper, and an envelope from a pigeonhole. As he turned back to face them however, the items fell out of his hand, and when he gathered them up and handed them over, the slips had increased to three.

"We missed you at lunch," he went on. "Did you enjoy your outing?"

Ada, who had not missed a thing, kept her voice steady as she replied, "Yes, but I have a slight headache now. I think a nap will do me the world of good. Would it be possible to have some tea sent to my room?"

"Of course," he answered, his voice dripping with sugary sincerity.

The Major took a newspaper from a stand by the desk. "I'll see you at cocktail hour, Ada," and so saying, he walked away reading the headlines.

Riding in the lift to the second floor, Ada wondered if the Major's last statement was an intention or an assumption. Not that it mattered. No doubt he and the Wilson sisters would be in the lounge as usual.

She entered her room, put her hat & coat in the wardrobe, and checked that all was as it should be. Nothing had been disturbed and the bricks were still under the bed.

She went into the bathroom and washed her hands and face. "You're getting too old for this caper," she said to her reflection. There was a knock on the door. "Who is it?" she sang out.

"Travis with your tea."

She opened the door and clapped her hands when she saw the laden tray. "Oh, lovely. Some biscuits too. Custard creams - my favourites. Please thank Mr Ayres for me."

Mr Travis deposited the tray on the dressing table. "Ayres had nothing to do with it. He's such a skinflint, that he'd dole the sugar out granule by granule if he could. No, it was my idea. It's my way of apologising for yesterday when I was…um…upset."

Ada put a hand on his arm. "Never be ashamed of being honest. That way, there's little room for misunderstanding." She gave him her best smile. "Now, can you spare a moment?"

"Only just. Two of the kitchen staff have handed in their notice."

"I see. Well, I'll make it quick. There seems to be some confusion concerning Miss Davenport's knitting bag. Do you know what happened to it?"

"No. I don't think the police ever found it."

"Did any other possessions, either hers or those belonging to other guests, go missing?"

"It wasn't a burglary if that's what you're thinking. The police ruled that out straight away." He eyed her warily. "How did you know about the bag?"

"I told you yesterday that I was writing a book, and I can hardly come to Upper Markham without asking questions."

Once again Ada had applied the half-truth, half-lie maxim. It was not in her best interest to point out that his statement of yesterday had not included the fate of the bag.

"Is that how investigative journalists work?"

Ada shrugged. "I have no idea. I suppose each works in their own way. After our discussion yesterday, I did some thinking and had formed a theory about Miss Davenport's death, but this business about the bag has blown it out of the water." She sighed. "Oh, well, it was worth a try. Thanks for the tea and biscuits."

Mr Travis took the hint. He bowed and left the room, his expression inscrutable. In the corridor however, he glanced back at the door, uncertain if the woman in room 26 was really whom she claimed to be.

Ada poured a cup of tea, rummaged in her handbag, and swallowed two yellow pills. A few minutes later, the pain in her hip began to ease. She settled on the bed and read her messages.

Her name and room number were written on the envelope and the three slips of paper, one of which was slightly crinkled. The first message read, 'Mrs Brown telephoned at 10.38 am'. The second message was also from Florrie. This time it read, 'No trace as yet. Will keep digging'.

The third message was from Bert, and given its content, Ada was not surprised that Mr Ayres fount it curious. 'Sorry to tell you that William's best pair of rabbits have died.

Ada slowly shook her head. "Rabbits," she muttered, "couldn't he have invented something better?" She opened the envelope and extracted a single sheet of paper, unaware that not far away, hands were balled into white-knuckled fists.

***

What the hell is taking so long? Ha! The police are stupid. They will never know how close they came to catching me. Still, I must be careful. No more slip-ups, no more mistakes. God this waiting is driving me around the bend! I've got to do something. I'm tired of rotting in this hole. Hmm, who next? Silly question. It has to be...

Chapter 10. Revelations.

Ada reluctantly conceded that there was an artfulness to the vulgarity of the note, which tended to indicate that the writer possessed a high degree of intellect. But it was also the rambling of a lunatic. She put the note in her handbag, tore up the messages and put the pieces into the envelope, and going to the wardrobe, placed it inside her hat.

She glanced at the little travelling alarm clock. It was just after 2 pm. Her conversation with the Major had raised several questions, and to investigate further would involve going out again.

Though the pain in her hip had eased, she was hardly fit enough to dance a waltz let alone go running around town. All she could do was hope that the medication prescribed by 'Doc Mutton-Chops' would last for another hour.

***

Ada opened the door to the haberdashers, and as before, her nostrils were assailed by the smell of scented candles, potpourri, and fragrant oils. She made a pretence of browsing the shelves, and after selecting two antimacassars for appearances sake, approached the long wooden counter.

"Back again?" said the middle-aged woman who had served her that morning.

Ada adopted a sweet, slightly dotty persona, along with a posh accent that Florrie would have been proud of. "I couldn't believe it when I walked in here this morning. I was so enchanted that I just had to return. I do a lot of travelling, and I can tell you that there's not many shops like yours still in existence."

The woman laughed. "If I had a pound for everyone who's said that to me, I could have retired a long time ago."

"I'm Mrs Harris from The Larkspur in Pimlico."

"And I'm the proprietor, Mrs Osborne."

As they shook hands, Ada perceived a fault in her disguise. Considering she was supposed to be a genteel old lady, raised in an era where grace and charm were as inherent as manners, she was not wearing gloves. As Elizabeth Wilson had said, 'Women rarely went out without a hat and gloves'.

"You have many lovely things here," she continued. "I must tell my bridge club the next time we meet. Has the shop been here long?"

"Yes. My great grandfather established the business just after the war."

"How perfectly enduring. I'm staying at the Seabridge Hotel, which according to their brochure, has been in the same family for many years."

"Yes," replied Mrs Osborne, though without much enthusiasm. There were several unopened boxes on the counter, and it could not have been clearer that she was busy. Ada however, ploughed on.

"Well, I hope your shop survives a few more generations. I suppose with the redevelopment project, you'll be looking forward to all the new people coming to live here."

It seemed Ada had touched a nerve, for Mrs Osborne replied with asperity. "Not in the slightest. The development also includes two variety supermarkets, which no doubt will be crammed with cheap imports. Oh, I admit we're guilty of that too, but we have always taken pride in offering nationally made products.

"Take our linen for example. Most of it comes from Scotland or Ireland. In my opinion, nothing beats Irish cotton. But, it seems quality and durability are no longer relevant.

"Pardon my presumption, but you would be old enough to remember when young girls collected household items for their 'glory box' or 'bottom drawer'. They would spend hour's embroidering linen in preparation for marriage. Nowadays it's done by industrial machines."

Ada nodded in sympathy. "I know exactly what you mean. My Great Uncle Aljinon had his shirts tailer made for years. Then, when he was in his 90's, he discovered that for the previous 20 years he'd been wearing shirts partially made by machine. The shock almost killed him.

"As a matter of fact, Elizabeth Wilson and I were discussing the subject the other day. She too frowns on the new development. Do you know Miss Wilson?"

Mrs Osborne smiled as she replied, "Oh, yes. She used to come here with another lady who had taken up residence at the hotel. She didn't know anyone here, and so Miss Elizabeth took her 'under her wing'.

"And what a pair of scamps they were. Miss Elizabeth once put sneezing powder in a basket of potpourri. She thought it was a great joke."

Ada only just stopped herself from blurting out, 'You're kidding'. Elizabeth Wilson a scamp? Miss Katherine perhaps, for she'd shown yesterday that she enjoyed a good laugh, but her prim, hard-bitten sister play a joke?

But, was it really beyond the realm of possibility? Had not the Major repeated a comment made by Mr Ayres when they were in the trap - 'As a matter of fact, Ayres thinks the sisters are responsible'.

Ada pretended to look confused, which in reality was not far from the truth. "I have met Miss Katherine of course, but I don't think I've met the other lady."

"And nor will you," replied Mrs Osborne sadly. "She died under tragic circumstances, which is probably why Miss Elizabeth hasn't been here in months. I haven't seen her since…let me think…oh yes, since the day that murdered solicitor came here."

So far, Mrs Osborne had not mentioned Miss Davenport's name, and Ada was quite sure that, rather than evasive, the shopkeeper was being tactful. Nevertheless, she needed to confirm they were talking about the same person.

"Are you referring to a Miss Davenport?"

"Yes."

Ada sighed in lament. "Poor woman. I read about her death in a London newspaper." This was a relatively safe gambit. She had no idea if the spinster's demise had stretched beyond the borders of Upper Markham, and in all likelihood, neither did the shopkeeper.

Ada waited a moment for a response, and when none was forthcoming she 'cast a line'. "Strange that the solicitor came here. I mean, this is hardly an establishment for gentlemen."

"Exactly," said Mrs Osborne, taking the bait. "I wasn't here at the time, but Caroline remembered his visit because it was a hot day and he was wearing a 3-piece suit."

Ada raised an eyebrow. "Caroline?"

Mrs Osborne launched into an explanation of what Caroline McGuiness had seen and heard. Ada was willing to bet the deeds of her house that the police did not know about this witness. It also occurred to her that this was possibly the source of tension between the sisters - that Elizabeth was keeping schtum about seeing Alistair Walsh, whereas Katherine wanted her to come forward.

Mrs Osborne concluded, "Apparently, he didn't seem to know which of the old women was Miss Davenport. Not that anyone could blame him. They looked very much alike." She sniffed as she added, "Poor Mirabelle. If only Elizabeth had stayed with her. And to think it was my knitting needles that killed her."

"How do you know they were your needles? They could have come from anywhere."

Mrs Osborne shook her head. "I know because both ladies preferred metal needles to plastic ones, and I am the only person around here who stocks them."

"Elizabeth is a knitter?"

"And a very good one too. They made cardigans and jumpers and little toys, which I passed to the women's auxiliary. I thought Elizabeth would continue her charity work, perhaps even encourage her sister to take up knitting, but nothing came of it." She looked at Ada hopefully. "I don't suppose you'd like to knit something while you're staying at the hotel?"

Ada replied without thinking. "I wouldn't know one end of a knitting needle from the other."

Mrs Osborne looked at her curiously. "But you bought a pair of size 3 this morning, along with handkerchiefs and pillowcases."

Ada scrambled for an explanation. "Oh, the needles are not for me. My friend Mrs Brown also prefers metal needles." In truth, Florrie only possessed one knitting needle and a broken one at that. She used it to test when cakes and other homemade goodies were cooked.

Nevertheless, Ada gave silent thanks for her long time friend, and nor was it the first time. In the past, Florrie had mythically doubled as a secretary, a doctor, an entomologist, and an expert on the Ottoman Empire. And now to add to her repertoire, a knitter.

"Knitting is a dying art," commented the shopkeeper, showing signs of impatience. "Is there anything else I can help you with?"

Under her coat, Ada could feel the pain in her hip migrating from dull ache to threatening throb. She could not stay on her feet much longer. And yet she had to talk to Caroline McGuiness, primarily to discover why she hadn't come forward. Perhaps the girl had seen or heard something that had frightened her.

"That lamp on the top shelf over there. Could I take a closer look at it?"

"Certainly." Mrs Osborne fetched a pair of stepladders and began to climb up.

"Oh, please be careful," said Ada. "Where is your assistant? Get her to do it."

"I don't have one," replied Mrs Osborne, retrieving the lamp and returning to the counter.

The base was brown and the design indistinguishable, and Ada couldn't decide if it depicted three intertwined doves or two otters sitting on a rock.

Mrs Osbourne produced a cloth and began to wipe away the dust. "Look at the state of it," she complained. "Young people today think that jobs are as disposable as tissues. I've advertised for a replacement, but only two people applied and neither was suitable."

Ada was confused. "I'm sorry, my dear, but I don't quite follow. Are you saying Caroline doesn't work here anymore?"

"Yes. When Miss Davenport left the shop with the solicitor, she left her purchases here. Caroline was supposed to take them to the hotel the next morning, but she rang me complaining of a headache - no doubt the result of too much cider the night before, and so I took them there myself.

"The police were everywhere and I heard what happened to Miss Davenport. I returned to the shop at once and told Caroline all about it, and that's

113

when she explained about Miss Davenport and the solicitor.

"Naturally we were both upset and Caroline couldn't stop crying. She finished work that afternoon and I haven't seen her since. If you ask me, she's run away with a boyfriend."

"How very inconsiderate," said Ada sympathetically. With her gaze on the base she casually asked, "Did you tell the police about the solicitor coming here?"

The shopkeeper's amiability changed to superiority. "There was no point. I didn't witness anything, and after Caroline left me in the lurch, I wanted nothing to do with her. As far as I am concerned, the ungrateful girl can bury herself in the sand."

Ada was not a violent woman. Nevertheless, right at that moment, she could have picked up the lamp and smashed it to pieces. Mrs Osborne had withheld vital information because of selfish pride.

Ada took a steadying breath, anger superseding the pain in her hip. "I'm not sure about this lamp. I like the design but the colour is too dark for my taste. Well, goodbye for now, and thank you for the chat."

***

Ada was still angry when she returned to the hotel. She entered her room, checked that nothing had changed, slipped off her shoes, and lay on the bed. She rubbed her hip as she began to think.

The outing had garnered more information than expected, and Mrs Osborne's revelations had provided several avenues for enquiry. But on one point there was no doubt, to wit, that the Major and Elizabeth Wilson were hiding something, though whether it was the same secret was open to speculation.

Deciding there was nothing to be done for the time being, Ada settled down for a nap, and when she went downstairs at 5.30, the foyer was swarming with police.

Chapter 11. Lament.

Flashing blue lights bounced off the walls, and had it not been for the uniforms and white forensic suits, the foyer of the Seabridge Hotel would have resembled a 1970's disco.

Ada hurried into the cocktail lounge. The 40ish man and his young secretary were there, as was the couple in their 50's. As usual, the man was reading a book, and instead of garish yellow, the woman was wearing a vibrant red dress, which made the white bandage around her wrist stand out like a beacon. But the familiar tableaux was incomplete, for the Major and the sisters were missing.

After obtaining a soft drink, Ada sat at the 'Major's' table, which provided a clear view of what was happening outside. An ambulance and four police cars were blocking half the road, whilst uniformed officers using fluorescent batons were directing traffic away from the hotel.

In the reflection of the window, Ada saw the Major enter the lounge. He stopped, looked around, and then rushed to her side. "Ada," he whispered breathlessly, "I need your assistance urgently. Please come with me, there's been...erm... an accident," and without waiting for a response, he took her arm and propelled her out of the room.

He did not say a word as he guided her into the lift and pressed the button for the first floor. When the doors opened, Ada saw Mr Ayres and two policemen standing in the corridor. All three were talking in whispers.

The atmosphere was sombre as the Major guided her to room 16. He gently tapped on the door and opened it without invitation. Ada entered a room that was almost identical to her own, the main difference being that the bed was a single. A padded footstool reposed under the window, and Katherine Wilson was sitting in the armchair, her face buried in a man's handkerchief.

She raised her head and wailed, "She's dead, Ada. My sister is dead and I killed her!"

Stunned, Ada looked at the Major for confirmation. He slowly nodded and mouthed the word 'suicide'. Ada collected her wits and swung into action.

"Major, please go downstairs and fetch a brandy and a cup of sweet tea."

The old soldier left the room, and Ada looked for somewhere to sit down. The only chair was occupied, and to sit on the bed seemed disrespectful. She glanced at the footstool. There were some newspapers and a cardigan on top. She set them aside, brushed a sprinkling of talcum from a corner, and moved the stool closer to the weeping woman.

"What happened?" asked Ada, wiping her fingers on her dress.

Katherine took several shuddering breaths before replying, "My sister and I have been coming here ever since we were girls, and this dreadful redevelopment project is destroying those halcyon days.

"Yesterday morning, we decided to see the old pier while it was still standing, and when we saw you having breakfast with that horrible man, we thought to rescue you by inviting you to join us.

"Afterwards, when we returned to the hotel, Elizabeth was in a funny mood. She kept talking about our parents and the past. I think she was depressed."

Ada quickly reviewed the outing. While it was true Elizabeth had lapsed into bouts of melancholy, it was equally true that she'd previously demonstrated a strong self-will, unapologetically forthright in her opinions.

And yet Mrs Osborne had described her as a scamp. This opposing description of the same woman suggested that Elizabeth had suffered from some form of personality disorder. If this was the case then it would explain a great deal.

"She seemed alright last night," commented Ada.

"Yes, but I think she was pretending.

Just then, the Major knocked and entered. "The brandy and tea," he said quietly. "I brought a cup for you too."

He placed the tray on the dressing table and gave the brandy to Miss Katherine. She drank it in two gulps, giving no indication that she'd noticed his presence. Even so, Ada thought it prudent that he should leave, and when she jerked her head towards the door, he immediately acquiesced.

Having exchanged the brandy for the tea, Katherine's hands trembled as she held the cup. "After dinner last night," she resumed, "Elizabeth went to her room to write some letters. I knocked on her door about nine o'clock to see if she wanted a nightcap, but all she asked for was my sleeping pills. She sometimes took one, and so I gave her the bottle.

"When I knocked on her door for breakfast, she said she didn't want any. I came down alone just as you and the Major were leaving the hotel.

"When Elizabeth did not appear for luncheon, I began to grow concerned. It was only then that I tried her door. It was unlocked. I entered and saw her lying in bed. I thought she was asleep, but then I touched her hand." Her voice began to break. "She was ice-cold. The bottle of pills was on the nightstand and…oh, Ada, it was empty!"

She lapsed into a fresh paroxysm of weeping, the cup slipping out of her hand. Ada caught it just in time. She put the cup on the tray just as a nock sounded on the door. Thinking it was the Major with more bad news, she opened it at once.

Two uniformed officers flanked a plain-clothed detective. He was in his early 50's, tall and slender, with a lugubrious, heavy jowled face that gave him the look of a bloodhound. His Mackintosh looked relatively new but his Trilby was a throwback.

"Good evening," he said, raising his hat and speaking in a slow drawl. "I'm Inspector Raymond Butler and I want to speak to Katherine Wilson."

Ada spoke quietly. "I'm sorry, Inspector, but I don't think she's in a fit state to be interviewed. I've given her some tea and brandy but she's still very upset. Could it wait until later, perhaps even tomorrow?"

Her appeal fell on deaf ears. "And you are?" he enquired. Ada gave him a sanitised version of who she was and how she came to be there. "I see," he went on. "Well, as you are no doubt unfamiliar with police procedure, I will explain the position.

"Unlike some animals - elephants for example, the human memory is not infallible. Therefore, it is always best to speak to a witness while an event is still fresh in their mind. It can save trouble and ambiguity later."

"Inspector," she hissed, "I don't think she will ever forget the sight of her dead sister."

Katherine sniffed into the handkerchief as she said, "It's alright, Ada, I have been expecting them."

As Ada stepped back to allow them entry, she saw Mr Ayres standing near the door. 'Poor man', she thought. 'Two deaths in four months will not do much for the hotel's reputation'. She gave him a sympathetic smile and quietly closed the door.

Brushing past the officers, who seem to take up half the room, she resumed her seat and held the spinster's hand. "Is their anything I can do for you?"

Katherine started to shake her head and then stopped. "Yes, but only if it's not too much trouble."

"Of course not. What is it?"

The bereaved woman looked at the Inspector with puffy eyes. "Is my sister…I mean, is her…"

"Your sister was being placed in an ambulance just as I arrived. I assure you, she is being treated with the upmost dignity. Mr Ayres is present if you doubt my word."

"No. I'm sure you acted most properly." Katherine turned to Ada and pointed to the room next door. "There is a brown velvet jewellery box in the bedside drawer. Would you bring it to me?"

Ada started to rise but the Inspector held up a hand. "I'm sorry but I can't allow it. Your sister's room is a crime scene and must be preserved as is."

"I don't care! I have already lost my sister in this God forsaken place and I do not intend to lose her jewellery as well." Her eyes were almost popping out of her head, and once again Ada was reminded of what Florrie had said in the optometrist's - 'I look like a frog'.

There was a short silence, and then Inspector Butler gave Ada an affirmative nod. "Please do not touch more than you need to."

***

Ada turned on the light. Elizabeth Wilson's room was just as tidy as her sister's, and yet the evidence on the bedside table - the empty pill bottle, the pile of broken capsules, and all the fingerprint dust, seemed to mock its cleanliness. The scene could have been used as the front cover of a novel.

Without touching the bottle, Ada read the label - 'Take one tablet at night when required. H. Piccolo. Bayswater Medical Centre'. She made a mental note of the address and opened the bedside drawer.

There was the usual array of creams, handkerchiefs, nail scissors and the like. There were also bits of wool and several knitting patterns. Beneath these and perched on the hotel supplied writing portfolio was a brown velvet box.

Ada examined the portfolio first. There were several hand-written notes, predominantly knitting related. She scrutinised the handwriting for a moment, then returning the portfolio to the drawer, removed the jewellery box.

About five inches square, it contained pendants, watches, and brooches, many of them years old. There was also some 'chunky' costume jewellery that no modern woman would wear.

"Probably mementoes from her days in the theatre," murmured Ada, and closed the lid.

She tried to look at the ceiling fan but her vision was obscured by the light. She was in no condition for even a game of croquet, let alone perform acrobatics. Still, it had to be done. Her hip sent out a warning throb as she climbed on to the bed. She paused for a moment to gain her balance, and then ran her fingers along the topside of the blades.

Satisfied, she climbed down, straightened the rumpled coverlet, and returned next door.

Chapter 12. Lost & Found.

"Is this it?" asked Ada, resuming her seat and holding out the box. For answer, Katherine let out a strangled cry, and snatching the box with both hands, held it to her chest like a child hugging a beloved toy.

"I've sent for a doctor," said Inspector Butler quietly. "I'm sure he'll give her something to calm her down."

Ada was glad he had not said 'tranquiliser'. Perhaps he was not as insensitive as she'd first thought. When he next spoke however, the favourable reassessment of his character was instantly withdrawn.

"Thank you for your help, Mrs Harris, but you are no longer needed. You may go, but please do not repeat anything that was said." He addressed one of the constables. "Go downstairs and wait for the doctor."

Ada was furious at the dismissal, for she'd had no intention of leaving. However, having no authority nor familial reason to stay, she had no choice but to comply. She stood up and patted Katherine's shoulder.

"If you need me, no matter the reason, ring downstairs and they'll find me," and giving the Inspector a look of disapproval, she left the room.

***

Ada made a beeline for the cocktail lounge. Every head turned in her direction as she went to the bar. "I heard," said the bartender in a low voice. He poured a large whisky and pushed it into her hand. "On the house. You look like you need it."

She flashed him a grateful smile, and taking a deep drink, saw the Major approaching through the bottom of the glass. "Come with me," he said, and steered her towards the table by the window. "Is Miss Katherine alright?" he asked.

"Not really," she answered with a sigh. "But then, that's hardly unexpected."

The Major made overtures of sympathy and understanding, but Ada wasn't really listening. Indeed, she was so preoccupied with her thoughts, that when the Major revealed that he was in room 12 - four doors from the tragedy, she almost missed it.

He started to produce the newspaper and then stopped. "Perhaps not tonight," he said quietly, and returned it to his pocket. "Now, my dear, I know it's been a trying day but you must eat."

Ada tried to protest but he insisted. They went to the dining room and sat at their usual table. Ada, who normally enjoyed a robust appetite, ate very little and spoke even less. If the Major thought her solemnity perfectly natural, he was only half-right.

She was contemplating her next move, which involved making several phone calls. Dare she use the phone in her room? It crossed her mind that perhaps the Inspector would co-operate. But, no. It could raise some awkward questions that she was not prepared to answer. There was no choice. She would have to go out again.

"I'm sorry, Major, but I'm not good company tonight." She smiled wanly and stood up. "I think I'll go for a walk."

The Major also stood up. "Well, if you'll give me a minute to get my coat, I'll come with you. It's very dark outside. I think we're in for a storm."

Ada held up a hand, her tone determined. "No, thank you, Major. I would prefer to be alone. I'll catch up with you later."

She hurried to her room, donned her hat and coat, and quickly exited the hotel, not bothering to leave her key at the desk. However, the Major was not the only person to see her leave.

**

A strong wind was blowing off the ocean, the whitecaps churning with discontent. Walking rather quickly, but not so fast as to attract attention, Ada made her way to the phone box, pausing once when she almost lost her hat.

Much to her satisfaction, the interior light was broken, meaning that she could proceed relatively unobserved. At the conclusion of the call, she lingered to consider the information she'd been given, and perhaps more importantly, what to do with it.

The 'job' was proving more difficult than expected. However, one fact had been established beyond doubt. The hand-written note she'd received earlier that day, and which was still secreted in her handbag, had not been written by Elizabeth Wilson prior to her death. The handwritten knitting notes in the portfolio proved it. Besides, even though the elderly spinster had been forthright to the point of dictatorial, vulgarity was an anathema to her nature, and whoever had written the note was certainly an expert on the subject.

Ada exited the box. "What a blore," she muttered, applying a 'perky' word to the weather. She had intended to make the return journey a leisurely if wind swept stroll, but the large raindrops that began to fall persuaded her otherwise.

She walked quickly towards the hotel, the lights in the portico shining like beacons. Just before crossing the road, she removed the envelope from her hat, tore it to shreds like the messages therein, and let the wind do the rest. A short distance away, a dark clad figure hiding behind a parked car, watched her with murderous eyes.

***

Mr Ayres was behind the reception desk, and upon seeing her enter the hotel, dramatically clutched his chest. "Oh, where have you been? You gave me an awful fright."

"I did?"

He pointed to the ceiling and whispered, "Given the unfortunate event upstairs, when I didn't see you in the cocktail lounge after dinner, I thought something had happened to you."

He produced a handkerchief and made a great show of mopping his brow. Ada tried not to laugh.

His exaggerated display was both comical and transparent. Nevertheless, she decided to indulge his whim.

"Thank you for your concern, but as you can plainly see, I am perfectly fine. I just needed some fresh air. It's been a very trying day. I'm sure you understand."

"For us all," he quipped. "Would you like some tea sent to your room?"

Ada was glad he'd mentioned it, for she wanted to talk to Mr Travis again. "Actually, some nice milky coffee would go down a treat."

Mr Ayres opened his mouth to speak but Ada did not give him chance. She quickly went to the lift. She did not want a lecture on why she should leave her key behind. More to the point, she did not want to encounter the Major. Though his compassion and understanding had been genuine, she was still not ready to eliminate him as a suspect.

***

Ada deposited her damp hat and coat in the wardrobe, then opening the bedside drawer, removed a sheet of hotel stationery from the writing portfolio. She then extracted the offending note from her handbag and compared the two. Apart from the top printed portion which had been torn off, the paper was identical.

"Ada, you're slipping," she rebuked, and returned both items to their places.

She sat on the edge of the bed and with uncharacteristic impatience, waited for Mr Travis to arrive. Not only did she have specific questions for him, but given that Miss Elizabeth's death was the second in the hotel within months, she wanted to know the mood 'below stairs'.

When there was a tap on the door, she opened it at once. Her welcoming smile slipped off her face. It was not the valet but Mr Ayres.

"This is very good of you," she said graciously, trying to hide her disappointment. "Is Mr Travis not on duty tonight?"

"Travis has terminated his employment," he answered, placing the tray on the dressing table.

"He quit?" she shrilled in surprise. Realising she'd expressed too much concern, she emitted a cough and threw in several sneezes for good measure. "Oh, please excuse me," she went on nasally, "it must be the damp night air. I hope I haven't caught a chill.

"Now, what were we talking about? Oh yes, Mr Travis. So, he's gone. It must be a great loss to you."

Mr Ayres turned to face her, and for the briefest of moments, his expression of disapproval mirrored that of the late Elizabeth Wilson. "As you say, he quit. We shall miss him of course, and it will take some time to find a suitable replacement. Therefore, I apologise in advance if future service is a little slow."

Though his statement had been courteous and appropriate, his tone implied that he couldn't care less. Where was the caring sharing host of a few minutes earlier? Once again Ada recalled what the Major had said – 'his moods swing like a monkey through the trees', and changed tack to mild curiosity.

"Oh, what a pity. When I saw him earlier today, he never said anything about it. When did he leave?"

"At the conclusion of his shift." Mr Ayres looked at her warily. "Why are you so interested?"

"Oh, no reason," she replied airily. "He was an efficient young man and a delight to talk to. I hope you'll give him a good reference."

Mr Ayres gave a single nod, and whether by accident or design, copied Ada's action in the foyer, in that he quickly left the room as if not wanting to be questioned.

Ada was not sure if she believed in premonition, for she had witnessed too many supposed coincidences to dismiss it entirely. Nevertheless, as she stood in the middle of the room, the hair on her arms stood on end. Indeed, such was the creepiness, that she dipped a finger into the coffee and cautiously tasted it.

Her gaze fell on the ceiling fan above the bed. She placed the cup on the nightstand and performed the same manoeuvre as in Elizabeth's room. The result was identical - dusty, greasy fingers.

Climbing off the bed, her hip sent a none-to-subtle message that it had been working hard all day. Ada took the hint. She swallowed two tablets, soaked in a hot bath, and lamented her luck.

Two sources of information had been lost, and she doubted if Katherine Wilson would be in her right mind any time soon. Perhaps more importantly, was it just coincidence that the valet had resigned on the same day another guest had been found dead?

"I'll think about it in the morning," she murmured as she pulled out the plug. The noise of the draining water obscured a second sound - that of a door being opened and closed further down the corridor.

***

This killing lark gets easier every time. Perhaps when everything's settled, I'll go into business for myself. Once again I've got the police running around like cretins. God but they're stupid. Don't they know how easy it is to fake a suicide? Hmm, better make the next one an accident. Don't want to push my luck.

Chapter 13. Aftermath.

The following morning in the dining room, only the sound of chinking crockery disturbed the respectful silence. Given that she'd eaten very little the night before, Ada was ravenous. She was on her second cup of tea when the Major entered and joined her.

"Good morning, my dear," he said in a subdued voice. "I hope you weren't too upset last night and managed to sleep alright."

"Morning, Major. Unfortunately, I did toss and turn a little, but I suppose that's only to be expected." In truth, she'd slept like a log.

The Major excused himself, obtained his breakfast, and returned to the table. "What are your plans for today?" he asked while spreading a generous amount of butter and marmalade on a slice of toast. If he was following a diet then it was doomed to failure.

Ada sighed in lament. "Before yesterday's tragedy, I had intended to explore the old end of the foreshore again. But, under the circumstances, a day of frivolity seems inappropriate."

"Nonsense," he said robustly, his voice penetrating the gloomy silence. Only a blind person could have missed the glances of disapproval cast in his direction. He lowered his voice and continued, "Yes last night's event was tragic, but it doesn't mean you have to stop living.

"After what you told me in the trap yesterday, I regret not being able to set Elizabeth straight. But, as she was nothing to me and vice versa, I'm not going to lose any sleep over her death. Would either sister weep for me if the situation was reversed? Of course they wouldn't."

Ada could not fault his logic. Even so, she still felt awkward about leaving the hotel. "Katherine probably feels alone and friendless, after all, she was devoted to Elizabeth."

The Major spoke reassuringly. "I thought you'd say something like that. Well, let me make two points. Firstly, I have just spoken to Mr Ayres, and he told me that Katherine is resting comfortably. He is personally keeping an eye on her.

"Secondly, you have to admit that Elizabeth was quite formidable. I don't wish to seem unkind, but perhaps in time, Katherine will come to appreciate her emancipation."

Ada understood the gist of his argument but did not entirely agree. She kept her opinion to herself as he went on, "Now, no more objections. What you need to shake off the doldrums is fresh air, distraction, and if you'll pardon the indelicacy, a good laugh. If you'll kindly wait till I've finished my breakfast, I shall endeavour to fill the prescription."

Ada looked at him curiously. Had he simply used the latter as a turn of phrase, or had he, like most killers, made an unconscious mistake? She weighed up the pros & cons, concluding that, as there was no way of knowing when she could question Katherine again, there was no point hanging around the hotel.

"You're right, Major," she said, glancing out the window. A bank of grey clouds was gathering in the distance. "Do you think it will rain?"

He studied the horizon, turning his head from side to side. He might have been watching a tennis match rather than judging the weather. "More than likely but probably not till this afternoon. If you have an umbrella or waterproof coat, I suggest you bring it just in case."

**

When breakfast was concluded, they rode in the lift to their respective floors. In her room, Ada put on a pair of stout walking shoes and her heavy coat, but before donning her hat, she employed a useful trick.

She plucked several hairs from her head and trapped them in the zip of the suitcase. The hair could not be dislodged unless the zip was pulled back. She verified that the bricks were still under the bed, looked around one more time, and exited the room.

The Major was flicking through a local newspaper when she arrived in the foyer. He looked rather distinguished in a camel coat and flat white hat, and Ada was sure he'd combed his moustache.

There was no sign of Mr Ayres, and after waiting a few minutes in case he should return, they put their keys on the desk and exited the hotel.

It was with a mixture of regret and frustration that Ada retraced her steps of two mornings ago. She showed no familiarity when passing the phone

133

box, and perhaps it was due to the inclement weather and her gloomy mood, but the booming music and flashing lights of the amusement arcade, seemed even more louder and brighter.

The strong wind of the previous evening had abated only slightly, and when Ada and the Major cleared the apex of the road, it hit them full in the face. Both had to grab their hats to prevent them from flying off.

The old pier looked even more helpless as the ocean smashed into the pylons, and in the near distance, an elderly man with shoulders hunched was trying to walk two dogs. On the pavement side, the huge yellow bollards, which had previously seemed solid and immovable, bent and rippled like paper.

Ada slowly looked around. What was it about this end of the foreshore that had caused Elizabeth's character to temporarily change? Her sudden burst of speed. Had she been running towards or away from something? If it had been nothing but a severe bout of melancholy as Katherine had stated, then why hadn't she also been affected? After all, it was Elizabeth herself who on Sunday evening, described her sister as 'highly strung'.

What, if anything, had any of it to do with Mirabelle Davenport and Alistair Walsh? Whilst it was true they had met in the haberdasher's, there was no other link between them.

In relation to the latter, one of last nights phone calls had revealed that Caroline McGuiness was not listed as a missing person. Even so, Ada had felt uneasy about the girl's disappearance and requested discreet enquiries be made.

Ada's train of thought was interrupted when the Major asked, "Are you alright? You look quite pensive."

On this occasion, she saw no reason to 'fudge' the truth. "I was thinking about Monday morning when I came here with the sisters. Elizabeth was quite upset at the state of the place. I asked her what it used to be like, and she became quite nostalgic when describing it."

"I know what she means," said the Major. "I remember walking along the pier, what with its gaily coloured stands and happy smiling faces. It was a lovely spot during summer, and it was not uncommon to find military rubbish in the sand.

"I was only about ten or twelve at the time, but even in the early 1960's, people were still trying to recapture pre-war graciousness and an uncomplicated existence. Regrettably, death and destruction claimed those too."

Ada felt a prickle behind her eyes. It was a great pity that the Major and Elizabeth did not settle their differences before she died. Ada pulled herself together. There was no time for sentiment. For better or worse, the Major was now her primary source of information.

"Elizabeth also spoke of graciousness when she mentioned a tearoom called Parkers. Does the name ring a bell?"

"Good gracious, so it does. It was directly opposite the pier and sold the most delicious scones." He leaned closer and whispered conspiratorially, "I know for a fact that servicemen in uniform received an extra dollop of jam."

"Really? Who told you that?"

"Oh...erm..." He suddenly became flustered and seemed to struggle to state a name. "My father," he finally said. "It's such a shame. This used to be such a lively place. Goodness knows what it'll be like when its finished.

"The redevelopment project reminds me of a voracious monster, devouring properties as it chews its way along the foreshore. This time next year, the place will be unrecognizable."

Ada did not immediately respond. The germ of an idea had just taken root. It was as impossible as it was ludicrous...and yet. She quickly changed the subject.

"You know," she said with an exaggerated shiver, "I don't think there's any point going further. Besides, the wind is playing havoc with my chilblains."

***

They retraced their steps, and upon reaching the amusement arcade, Ada stopped outside. "It's been years since I set foot in one of these. Do you mind if we go inside for a moment?"

If she'd have asked him to cut off his toes and cook them on a barbecue, he could not have looked more horrified. "Are you serious?"

"Oh, don't be such an old stick-in-the-mud. You said I needed cheering up. Come on, it'll be fun."

Even though the front of the arcade was completely exposed to the elements, the interior was surprisingly warm. It was also quite crowded. Computers flashed 'play me' type messages, and a bingo caller was applying his spiel.

"22 - two little ducks. Purse your lips, it's legs 11," which was followed by a chorus of wolf whistles.

Ada sat on a plastic chair in front of a car racing game, not to play it but to rest her hip. With all the walking and running around she'd done in the past few days, her pain threshold was practically zilch. 'At this rate', she thought, 'I'll need another holiday'.

Her medical self-diagnosis was curtailed by a massive clap of thunder. The shock wave reverberated through the floor, and for a few seconds, the music stopped and all the lights went out.

"I think," said the Major, turning up the collar of his coat, "we'd better make a run for it."

Run? That was the last thing she needed. "Would you mind if we stayed a little longer? My shoulder is rather sore today. Why don't we have a game of bingo?" His look of disgust supplied the answer.

They left the protection of the arcade. The wind was cruel and no respecter of age. Indeed, at one point when Ada was trying to prevent her hat from flying off, she lost her balance and would have fallen had the Major not grabbed her arm.

137

"I think it would be better if you clung onto me," he shouted above the gale. "I don't want any more accidents befalling you."

Ada hoped he meant this in a kindly way and not as a dire warning. She held on to his arm, and pushing the pain of her hip aside, matched his brisk pace.

There was another clap of thunder, and when the lightening lit up the thick leaden sky, the scene could have been taken from a Cecil B. De Mille biblical movie. The ocean heaved in angry swells, and it was only a matter of minutes, perhaps even seconds, before the heavens opened up.

***

Ada and the Major stood in the entrance to the hotel. Though their coats were speckled with raindrops, they had reached safety just in time. The amount of water pouring over the end of the portico was extraordinary. It was as if millions of buckets of water were being tipped out at once.

Mr Ayres was behind the reception desk, and to judge from his snarling expression, he was not best pleased. Nor did his mood improve when the lift opened and the 50ish woman, now wearing a black and red striped dress, marched across the foyer and banged her uninjured hand on the desk. It was hard to say which was the more furious - her face or the weather.

"Mr Ayres, what kind of a hotel are you running? My room is..." She stopped when she saw Ada and the Major, who were now waiting by the desk to collect their keys. "Oh, I do beg your pardon," she said apologetically. "Please, go ahead. A few more gallons of water in my room won't make any difference."

Mr Ayres made no comment as he slapped their keys on to the desk. The Major gently pulled Ada aside. "Would you like a brandy to warm you up?"

Ada recognised that the chances of cajoling Mr Ayres into bringing a tea tray to her room were practically nil, and whilst a stiff brandy would have gone down a treat, she wanted to keep a clear head. There was much to think about.

"No, thank you," she answered, taking a copy of the local paper from a stand by the desk. "If I don't have a little nap I won't be good for anything."

She crossed the foyer and entered the lift, and as the doors slowly closed, she saw that the Major still stood by the desk. He was not looking at anyone or anything, and yet there was a look of utter misery on his face.

***

Ada was thoughtful as she entered her room. Why had the Major looked so sad? Had she somehow thwarted a plan, or was it simply a case of loneliness? She wished Florrie would hurry with her enquiries.

Ada knew she would never love another man, and yet she was steadily being drawn to the Major. Was she also experiencing loneliness? Life without Frank had certainly been difficult, and since his death, her family had been a great comfort. But it had never occurred to her that, like the Major, she was actually on her own.

"Stop it," she rebuked, and hung her hat and coat in the wardrobe.

She checked the zip of the suitcase – the hair had gone. Once again she used the walking stick to feel under the bed. This time it did not touch anything. The bricks had also gone.

The travelling alarm clock showed 12.07 pm, and although hungry and choking for a cup of tea, Ada took two tablets, removed her shoes, and lay on the bed. She also practised relaxation techniques she'd learnt in India, and in more than one sense was relieved.

The Major could not have searched her room, at least not that morning, for he had the best alibi of all – herself. It occurred to her that perhaps he had an accomplice, but as he appeared more or less friendless, the possibility seemed remote. Nevertheless, for the time being at least, she had no choice but to tread cautiously.

Ada felt her eyelids droop, and as she settled down for a nap, something Florrie once said came back to her. 'You could find a mystery in a jigsaw puzzle'. "And that's what I have here," she mumbled into the pillow, "little pieces that on their own mean nothing. But, how to put them together so that they form a picture?"

Chapter 14. Dire Warning.

It was a nightmare and she knew it was, and yet she could not wake up. A bird was pecking her head. She could hear it but not feel it. The bird paused and then started again, this time more insistently.

Ada sat bolt upright. Someone was quietly knocking on the door. She climbed off the bed and approached the door cautiously, and a moment later she was staring at a drenched Mr Travis.

His cap was pulled low, and despite his pinched pink cheeks, which gave him a healthy glow, his expression was deadly serious. He put a finger to his lips and quickly closed the door.

"Forgive me for barging in on you, but I must speak to you urgently."

Ada pointed to the armchair. "Please, sit down."

Ignoring the invitation, he took a deep breath and gushed, "You must leave the hotel immediately."

"Why? Is the hotel on fire?" Her brain still a little drowsy, it took her a moment to fully wake up. "What are you doing here? I thought you'd resigned."

"No such luck - about the fire I mean, and as for me resigning, that's crap. Ayres sacked me after my shift yesterday, but that's not important right now. Please listen to me. Your life is in danger. You must leave at once."

In spite of his earnestness, Ada was not unduly perturbed. She had been expecting a turn of events, even though she did not know from which quarter they would originate. "There is no need to panic," she said calmly. "But, before you begin, give me your jacket and shoes."

He did as ordered. Ada went into the bathroom and hung his dripping jacket over the bath. She stuffed his shoes with towels and then returned to the room. "Now, tell me exactly what's happened."

"When I returned downstairs after bringing you the tea tray yesterday, Ayres asked what had taken me so long. I said that we'd been chatting, but of course, I didn't tell him the truth. Instead, I told him that we'd been talking about local places of interest."

"Good thinking," she responded. "Go on."

"At the end of my shift, he called me into the office and said that my services were no longer required. He had already written my wages cheque, including a month's severance pay. I asked him if I'd done anything wrong, to which he answered 'no'.

"The smarmy git wouldn't even look at me, but then, that's not so unusual for him. Anyway, I went for a drink to try and figure it out and then went home. The thing is, when I changed out of my work clothes, I saw that I still had my passkey."

Mr Travis was in full flow, and although anxious to hear his tale, Ada had to stop him. "What passkey?" she queried.

The ex-valet looked embarrassed as he explained, "It's a policy of the hotel that, should any guest ask about security, they are to be told that each room has only one key."

"Plus the master," chipped in Ada.

"Yes, but there are two copies of the master. I'm sorry I lied to you."

Ada flicked a wrist dismissively. "Forget it. Please continue."

"I thought that if Ayres discovered that I still had my passkey, he would stop the cheque - he's mean enough to do it. So, I decided to come back but couldn't get in. The police were everywhere, and when I asked an officer what had happened, he said there had been an accident.

"I went home again, and when I heard on the news what had really happened...well, I know it sounds daft, but something told me to return the passkey asap."

Ada nodded. "Gut instinct should never be ignored," she said sagely. "What did you do next?"

"Waited till the early hours of this morning and then came back. I used the kitchen entrance which is hardly ever locked. Thankfully there was nobody around, including Ayres. I went behind the desk to write him a note and put the key in an envelope. By the way, the mirror between the pigeonholes is a two-way."

"I'd guest as much. Its position is a little too obvious. Nobody would put a mirror there without a reason."

"Thing is, I heard him talking on the phone in his office. I suppose he was moving about because his voice kept fading in and out. I didn't hear much because all I wanted to do was leave the key and get out of there.

"He said, 'don't be stupid, another one now will cause more suspicion'. Then he said, 'that old bag,

Harris, has been asking questions'." He paused and looked at her apprehensively. "The last thing I heard him say was, 'leave it to me, I'll get rid of her'."

Outwardly, Ada was the epitome of calm. Inwardly, she was tingling with anticipation, for although there was more of the story to come, certain pieces of the 'jigsaw puzzle' had fallen into place.

"It made my blood run cold," he continued. "I took off. I didn't know what to think, but the one thing I knew for sure was that I had to warn you.

"I didn't dare risk leaving you a message, and so I set my alarm for six o'clock. But, I...um...slept in. Anyway, when I finally managed to sneak in and knock on your door, there was no answer.

"I used the passkey to enter and waited a few minutes, hoping you were finishing breakfast, and when you didn't show up, I checked the wardrobe. Your hat and coat were gone, and I guessed you'd already gone out.

"I sneaked out and began searching the foreshore. I looked in every place I could think of. I even went to that haberdashery shop, but the woman behind the counter said she hadn't seen you since yesterday.

"I came back again and was prepared to wait in another room all day, but fortunately you'd returned in the interim." He let out a relieved sigh and slumped back in the chair. "End of report."

Ada had never felt so humble in her life, and even though it was an appalling lack of gratitude to exploit his heroism, she now had no choice. "I would like to ask you more questions about Miss

Davenport, and as you are no longer an employee of the hotel, I presume you can answer honestly."

"I have no loyalty to Ayres. In a way, I'm glad he sacked me, though admittedly, given the size of Upper Markham, my employment prospects look pretty grim."

Ada was not so sure about this. He was an intelligent, sharp young man who could possibly be 'recruited'. It was worth considering, but not at the moment. "In which room was Miss Davenport killed?"

"Number 36." He pointed at the ceiling. "Directly above this room."

"What happened to her belongings?"

"The police have them."

"Did they take everything in her room?"

"I believe so."

Ada knew her next question might upset him. Nevertheless, it had to be asked. "Did you see her body?"

Mr Travis shivered and not because of his damp clothes. "No."

"Did she pay her bill regularly?"

"I presume so. I had nothing to do with the accounts."

"And when did the practical jokes begin?"

"Hmm…about five or six months ago."

"Which guests arrived about that time and are still here?"

Mr Travis thought for a moment and then counted them off on his fingers. "The Wilson sisters have been here the longest, followed by the Major and then Miss Davenport. Mr Tomlinson and his secretary arrived about a week later."

"I've seen them several times, and quite frankly they look out of place. She is definitely not the secretarial type, and his clothes suggest that he'd be much more at home in the Ritz or the Dorchester. Do you know why they're here?"

Mr Travis grinned roguishly. "Well, I don't know about her, but he's involved in the redevelopment project. Here, I'll show you."

He opened the local newspaper that Ada had picked up earlier. He flicked through the pages and indicated a photograph. It was black & white and quite grainy, and showed two men looking at a large map of the area. The caption underneath read, 'Representatives of the redevelopment project studying the plans for the new foreshore'. The features of one man were clearly visible, while the other had his back half turned to the camera.

Mr Travis pointed to the second man. "That's Tomlinson. You can't see him properly but it's definitely him."

Ada scrutinised the picture for a moment and then went on, "How long have you worked at the hotel?"

"Just under a year."

"Do you know who your predecessor was?"

"Yes, it was Joe Macdonald." The ex-valet suddenly became thoughtful. "Now, isn't that strange? When Ayres first hired me, what with all the running around and stuff, he said he needed a younger man because Joe, who is in his 50's, couldn't do the job.

146

"At the time, I thought this made sense because I knew Joe suffered from varicose veins. But when I saw him a few months later, he told me that, rather than being let go on the grounds of his health, he had been sacked for incompetence."

Ada had one more question - at least for the present, and one that was very important to her. "Do you still have the passkey?"

Mr Travis gave her a boyish grin as he withdrew it from his pocket. But, rather than elated, Ada became serious. "I cannot thank you enough for what you did today. Now I must ask you to help me again. Will you do it?"

He looked into her soft blue eyes. He knew that her questions had not been asked at random or from curiosity. They had been too specific. "Who are you, Mrs Harris? And please don't tell me you're an author because…well, I just know you're not."

She gave him her warmest 'grandmotherly' smile. "I can't tell you that, but I will say this much, your help will not go unnoticed or unrewarded." She did not give him time to decipher her cryptic reply. "Now, please pay attention. I have a very important task for you. Firstly, do you have a car?"

"Yes - it's parked in the back lane."

"Very good. Now, leave the hotel by the foyer and don't worry if Mr Ayres sees you. You no longer work here and therefore are not subject to his employment rules. Go to the council offices and find out who owns the amusement arcade."

"Oh, I don't need to go anywhere for that. I can tell you now its Colin Macdonald."

"Macdonald? Same surname as your predecessor?"

"Same surname, same family - they're brothers."

"And Colin Macdonald actually owns the arcade?"

"Well, he runs it and has done so for several years."

Ada shook her head. "No, you don't quite understand. I want to know who owns the building and the land it's sitting on."

Mr Travis checked his watch. "It's quarter to three and I think the municipal offices shut at 4.30. If I hurry, I should be able to find out."

"There might be a little more to it. If the land is owned by a company, you will need to backtrack even further. Dig as deep as you can, but I must know who the actual owner is. Come here at 11 o'clock tonight, and for goodness sake don't lose that passkey."

He grinned. "No chance."

Retrieving his shoes and jacket, which were still rather wet, Ada helped him put them on. "You know, sneaking in and out of the hotel like that was very brave of you."

"Not really," he answered, adjusting his soggy collar. "I used the backstairs."

Ada gaped at him, her astonishment genuine. "What backstairs? I haven't seen them."

"No, you wouldn't. During World War II, the military took over the hotel for a while because they wanted a safe place to hide some Nazi defectors.

When the military left, much to old Mr Ayres's surprise, he had a new set of stairs.

"The rooms marked 19, 29, and 39, are false. The backstairs is behind them."

"I don't remember reading anything about this in the hotel brochure. How do you know the story of the stairs?"

"Miss Davenport rang down for some tea. I took up a tray, and when I entered her room, she was playing cards with Elizabeth Wilson.

"While we were chatting, Miss Davenport asked if I'd used the backstairs, and when I said I had, she asked if I knew how they came to be built.

"I said I didn't, and so she told me the story. She said the operation was called 'Waterloo'. I remember because I associated the name with ABBA."

"When was this?"

"I think she said 1945."

Ada chuckled. "No, not the stairs. When did she tell you the story?"

"Oh," he said with a sheepish grin, realising his mistake. "It was roughly about a week before she died."

Though Ada remained calm, in her mind, another piece of the puzzle had slotted into place. "Has Mr Ayres or anyone else ever told you the story of the stairs?"

"Not that I can remember."

"Where is the main access point?"

"In the kitchen. Now, I'd better be off if you want that information tonight. See you at eleven."

He gave her a quick military salute and slipped out the room.

"I hope he'll be alright," she murmured as she locked the door.

While it was true the valet's appearance had caught her by surprise, it was equally true that the information he had imparted was of tremendous value. The 'jigsaw', whilst not exactly taking shape, was beginning to have substance.

She needed a cup of tea. She was just contemplating going downstairs when there were two loud knocks on the door. Her heart skipped a beat. Had something gone wrong already? She darted across and without enquiring her visitor's name, opened the door. It was not the valet.

Chapter 15. Fishing.

Once again Ada was caught off guard. "Oh, Inspector Butler. How nice to see you again."

The Inspector stood in the doorway, rain running down his Mackintosh and dripping on the floor. "Good afternoon, Mrs Harris. May I have a word with you?"

"Of course."

As she stepped back to allow him entry, she realised she was not wearing shoes. While she could never have matched Elizabeth Wilson for primness, it did seem less than courteous to be interviewed by the police in stocking feet.

She moved to the side of the bed, and using a foot, surreptitiously felt around until it connected with her slippers. "Please, sit down," she invited, her feet now encased in woolly tartan.

If the Inspector noticed the pantomime, he gave no sign as he sat in the armchair and consulted a notebook. "Just a few routine questions," he said, trotting out the standard introduction. "I understand you had drinks with the Wilson sisters on Sunday evening."

Ada decided to play it straight – at least for now. "Correct."

"Did you know the sister's before coming to the hotel?"

"No."

"How did you meet them?"

"I didn't know anyone when I arrived, and as they were the only persons of my age in the cocktail

151

lounge, I introduced myself. They invited me to join them."

"And what did you talk about?"

Ada shrugged. "Nothing much - just three old ladies having a chat."

"Yes, but what did you actually discuss?"

Ada was conservative with the truth. "Movies, holidays, and knitting patterns."

"Is that all?"

"If you expect me to recall every word then I'm afraid I must disappoint you."

Inspector Butler wrote in his notebook and then said, "I understand from Mr Ayres, that you and Major Eaton went out together yesterday morning, and upon returning, you came directly to your room."

"Yes. I ordered tea, which duly arrived, and then took a nap. I awoke just before five o'clock and went downstairs to the cocktail lounge. The Major entered about five minutes later and told me there'd been an accident."

"The Major told me that he couldn't find you beforehand."

The statement and tone contained a hint of accusation. Ada defused both and his momentum by applying simple logic. "That, Inspector, depends on where he was looking. As far as I am aware, Major Eaton does not know which room is mine. If he had, no doubt he would have knocked on my door. But,, as I was already in the lounge, your point is mute."

When the Inspector looked uncomfortable and shifted in his chair, Ada was pleased she'd rattled him. She wanted him to hurry up and leave, for there was still a chance that Mr Travis might return. The Inspector, however, was frustratingly dogged.

"In the short time you knew Elizabeth Wilson, did you get the impression that she was suicidal?"

Ada answered with absolute conviction. "Not in the slightest."

"Just out of curiosity, how long have you known Major Eaton?"

"I met him for the first time on Sunday evening."

"Nice chap?"

"Very amiable."

"A joker?"

His tone was more conversational than interrogatory, and yet Ada wasn't buying it. 'So', she thought, 'that's the way the wind's blowing'. She deliberately misinterpreted his meaning.

"He likes a good laugh if that's what you mean."

"Why do you think he requested your assistance last evening? After all, you'd only just met."

Half-serious, half-deliberate, Ada let out a sigh of exasperation. "Older people have a tendency to gravitate towards each other. I suppose the Major thought Katherine Wilson would more easily accept the comfort of a woman nearer her own age than someone younger."

"When you entered Miss Elizabeth's room to retrieve the jewellery box, did you notice anything unusual?"

153

Ada started to feel resentful. While she appreciated that he had a job to do, he was asking her questions he already knew the answers to.

"As I had never been in her room before, I can't honestly say. Katherine would be the best person to ask. Have you seen her today?"

"Yes."

"Is she well enough for a visitor?"

"She is a little better, but I would advise you to see her before tomorrow morning. She is leaving the hotel."

This was both news and a blow. Ada kept her voice steady as she remarked, "Yes, I don't think she'll want to live here now. Have you any idea where she's going? I'd like to keep in touch with her."

"She said she has some cousins in Wales and is going to stay with one of them for a while."

Ada phrased her next question as a statement. "Perhaps I should help her pack. It won't be easy for her."

"Not a pleasant task." He stood up. "Well, as you were asleep at the time, I daresay you can't tell me anything of use."

Ada pretended to consider the point. "Not off the top of my head, but if you give me your phone number, I'll ring you if I think of anything."

He gave her a business card as she escorted him to the door. 'Poor lamb', she thought, 'he hasn't got a clue. I'll give him a hint'.

"Inspector, I understand it was Elizabeth Wilson who found the body of Mirabelle Davenport."

He looked at her sharply. "How do you know that if you've only been here a few days?"

Ada answered airily. "Oh, someone mentioned it, or perhaps I overheard it in the dining room."

The Inspector rubbed his chin. "Your information is correct. What of it? Have you heard something?"

Ada resisted the urge to laugh. She could have spent the next hour telling him what she knew. Instead, she adopted the persona of a gossipy old lady. "Not exactly, but don't you think it rather odd that Miss Davenport died, and the person who found her is now dead?"

She thought of adding, 'and both women saw Alistair Walsh on the day he died', but thought this a step too far. The last thing she wanted was for the police to start investigating her own activities. Besides, for all the Inspector's supposed groping in the dark, she did not underestimate his ability.

"I wouldn't read too much into that," he answered. "It's probably just coincidence. Thank you for your assistance – good afternoon."

He raised his hat and left the room, and in spite of his dismissive response to her innuendo, as he walked away, his quick pace and stiff shoulders were suggestive of bloodhound in search of a scent.

***

Ada immediately sprang into action. She swapped her slippers for shoes, placed more hair in the zip of her suitcase, and left her room. Three minutes later she tapped on the door to room 16.

"Who is it?" said a feeble voice.

"Ada. May I come in?"

The door slowly opened to reveal a forlorn looking Katherine Wilson. "Come in," she said feebly. Her gait was little more than a shuffle, and she was stooping as if she had the weight of the world on her shoulders. She wearily sat in the armchair, a handkerchief clutched in her hand.

Ada closed the door as she said, "I came to see how you were feeling, and if there was anything I could do for you."

She sat on the bed, the footstool being covered with a pile of clothes. It was the only item out of place, and yet it lent an air of untidiness to the spotless room.

"Thank you," replied Katherine, "but I think everything is in hand. The police have been extremely considerate, as has Mr Ayres.

"I have decided to leave in the morning and stay with a cousin in Wales, and Mr Ayres has offered to pack our belongings and send them on."

"That must be a great comfort to you. Have you contacted your cousin? I can phone them if you wish."

Katherine shook her head. "I have made all the necessary arrangements."

"Have you eaten anything today? Would you like me to accompany you to the dining room?"

"No! No! No!" Katherine let out an anguished cry. The hand clutching the handkerchief, flew to her neck as though she was being choked.

Ada could not understand the reaction. It then occurred to her that, suggesting a routine that had previously included the deceased sister, was too much of a reminder, even though well intentioned.

Ada was about to apologise when Katherine beat her to it. "I am very sorry, Ada. That was unforgivable of me. Mr Ayres made a similar suggestion a little earlier and I reacted the same way. I can never enter that dining room again. He mentioned something about sending up a tray, but to be honest, I'm not hungry. I do thank you for thinking of me."

They lapsed into a stilted silence, broken only by the ticking of an unseen clock. Ada felt awkward and superfluous. "Well, if you're sure there's nothing I can do for you, I'll leave you in peace. I'll see you in the morning before you leave."

She was at the door when Katherine said, "Thank you for yesterday. You were of great comfort to me. I'm sure my sister, wherever she is now, will appreciate it."

"Think nothing of it," said Ada, and quietly closed the door behind her.

She walked to the end of the corridor and was about to press the button for the lift when she suddenly stopped. The hair on her arms had stood on end again. Was it another premonition? Was Mr Travis in trouble? Should she have left Katherine alone?

Glancing to her right, she saw she was opposite the fake room 19. She went across and tried the handle. It was locked. Then, as she moved away, a faint noise reached her ears. It sounded like someone had stepped back behind the door and scraped a shoe on a wall.

Chapter 16. Truth & Lies.

Ada exchanged her shoes for slippers and anxiously paced the room. Something – an idea, a thought, a suggestion was bordering on fruition. But, whatever was knocking on the door of her conscience could not gain admission.

"Oh, come on - think!" She stamped her foot and looked out of the window.

The weather now lashing the seaside town was what forecasters called 'filthy'. The streets were completely deserted, and in the near distance, a fishing vessel was ploughing through the churning ocean, its running lights twinkling like tiny jewels.

Ada suddenly stiffened. A 'penny' had just dropped. "Of course! Why didn't I think of it before? An abditory."

She turned and glared at the phone by the bed. If she didn't want to catch pneumonia then she would have to risk using it. Retrieving the Inspector's card, she dialled his number and held her breath.

It seemed to take an eternity before he finally answered. "Yes, Mrs Harris? What can I do for you?"

"Good evening, Inspector," she said in what she hoped was an affable voice. "I wonder if you would mind settling a point that's bothering me."

"And that is?"

"I believe you still have Miss Davenport's personal effects."

There was a slight pause before he answered, "You are remarkably well informed."

"Not really. I mean, isn't it usual for the police to retain effects when no next of kin can be found?"

"The disposal of an unclaimed deceased's property varies from county to county, but yes, you are correct. Miss Davenport's property is still here."

Ada bit her lip. She could not keep his suspicion at bay much longer. "Can you tell me if she owned anything valuable - a rare book or a painting for example?"

"No. Quite the contrary in fact. For a woman of her age, she had very few possessions. They fit into one large suitcase."

"Are you absolutely sure about that?" she asked insistently.

"Very sure." As expected, a note of suspicion crept into his voice. "Why do you ask?"

Ada gripped the receiver even tighter as she announced, "Because I think Miss Elizabeth's murder is connected to that of Miss Davenport."

Inspector Butler let out an exasperated sigh. "You're jumping the gun. Elizabeth Wilson hasn't been autopsied yet."

"Nevertheless, there is no doubt in my mind that she was murdered." Ada took a deep breath. 'Here goes', she thought, 'sink or swim'. "And both women saw Alistair Walsh the day he died."

There was a long pause at the other end of the phone. Finally, he asked, "Have you seen Miss Katherine yet?"

"Actually, I've just come from her room."

"And how did she seem to you?"

"Still upset but calmer than yesterday."

159

"That's not really surprising. The doctor gave her something to sleep last night and left some tranquilisers for today. I was in the room at the time. She balked at taking them but he insisted."

With sinking heart, Ada realised that, not only had he dismissed her dramatic statement, but that he was humouring her. It was times like these when she missed her husband. If he was not engaged on a 'job', they would toss a problem around and more often than not, find a solution. Now there was nobody with whom she could discuss her work, except of course, Florrie.

And then reality struck like lightning. Being preoccupied with murder, she had forgotten about Florrie's comments on the phone. The big question was, how much did her faithful friend actually know?

Ada shook her head. She must not be distracted by personal issues. Any problem back home would have to wait till she returned. Conjecture was pointless. Right now it was time for affirmative action.

"Inspector, I know you've probably had a long day, and I don't want to impose on you, but would you meet me in the cocktail lounge at 9.30? You will not be wasting your time."

Inspector Butler rubbed his tired eyes. The weather was atrocious and his faculties were not at their best. He considered the invitation. Did she know something or was she guessing? It would only cost a drink to find out.

"Certainly," he answered. "I'll see you at 9.30."

***

In room 26, Mrs Harris produced her notebook and began to make a list. At the police station, Inspector Butler sat in thought and then made several phone calls. In the hotel kitchen, preparations were well underway for dinner, while in room 12, Major Eaton brushed the jacket and trousers he would wear that evening. In room 16, Miss Katherine sat wide-eyed and fearful, while at the reception desk, Mr Ayres was absent from his post.

***

Ada was so engrossed in her notes that when the phone beside the bed rang, she jumped. "Yes?"

It was Mr Ayres. "Mrs Harris, I have a Mr Eagles on the line. Will you accept the call?"

Ada was instantly alert. Even so, she kept her voice steady as she responded, "Yes - put him through."

There were two clicks and then Bert said, "Hello, Ada. How are you?"

"Bonjour, Bert. How nice of you to call. How are the children?"

"Fine. How's your holiday?"

"Somewhat eventful."

"Same here. Did you get my message about William's rabbits?"

"Yes," she said slowly, her voice sounding appropriately sorrowful. "How did they die?"

"As far as we can tell, from natural causes."

"Surely William can back-track? After all, they were pedigree."

"That's what everybody thought, but it turns out they weren't. We checked the papers and found two males and one female. None ever bred, and the details of the mother of the males are missing."

"Oh, dear. William must be devastated."

"Yes, he is, but I'm sure he'll find another hobby. So, are you enjoying yourself?"

"The food is surprisingly good, and until today, so was the weather. It's now turned nasty."

Bert laughed. "Typical English weather. I think summer was on a Friday this year."

They talked for a few more minutes and then said 'goodbye'. No sooner had Ada hung up when the phone rang again. "My but you're popular tonight," said Mr Ayres. "I now have a Mrs Brown on the line. Will you take the call?"

"Yes."

Two clicks and then Florrie said, "Ada?"

"Yes."

"Got a pen?"

Ada reached for her notebook which was still on the bed. "Go ahead."

"Charles Edward Eaton, born Oxford, 21st October 1952. Two siblings - Peter and Phillipa, both deceased, as are the parents."

"Excellent. Anything else?"

There was a distinct pause before Florrie answered, "Ada, he's not trying to chat you up or anything like that, is he?"

Ada laughed. "Are you kidding? Who would look at an old fossil like me?"

Again, Florrie hesitated. "Ada, I found something a bit funny."

"What?"

"Before I answer, were you aware that someone died in that hotel a few months ago? A woman named Mirabelle Davenport?"

Ada tried to remain calm. "It's been mentioned. What of it?"

"Well, you'll never guess who her aunty was."

"Who?"

Florrie dropped her 'bomb'. Ada could hardly speak for excitement. She quickly consulted her notes and then said, "Could you look up something else for me?"

There was the sound of a clicking keyboard before Florrie replied, "You only have to command, mem sahib."

***

What the hell is she playing at? Who is she? Why is she here? Has someone sent her? I've not waited all this time just to have my plan thwarted by a hag! She has to go! No knitting needles or tablets this time. She'll suffer for her interference - I'll make sure of that.

***

With a nonchalance that was entirely false, Ada strolled into the cocktail lounge. All the 'regulars' except Katherine Wilson were seated at their usual tables. Ada stood at the bar and while waiting to be

163

served, used its rear mirror to study the man in his 40's.

Mr Tomlinson was impeccably dressed as usual, with an all-over tan that was probably fake. Ada then looked at the 50ish woman. Tonight she was wearing arguably the ultimate fashion accessory. Her injured wrist was now wrapped in a blue satin bandage that matched the colour of her dress.

"Whiskey?" inquired the bartender, giving her a looked that said, 'as if I need ask'.

Ada reluctantly abstained. She trusted her instincts, and there was definitely 'something' in the wind. She obtained a soft drink and joined the Major, who was gazing out of the window.

"What a night," he commented. "You would have to be mad or have a good reason to go out on a night like this."

"I don't remember the brochure offering a severe thunderstorm as an attraction," she said with a chuckle, trying to keep the mood light. It was vital that she maintain an appearance of normality.

But the Major barely smiled. He seemed quite distracted, and Ada wondered if he wanted to be alone. As though sensing her uncertainty he asked, "Did you get a visit from the police?"

"Yes. Inspector Butler came to see me this afternoon. He asked a few general questions and then left."

"Same here." The Major turned away from the window and looked at her directly. "But you know what strikes me as odd? I learned today that it was Miss Elizabeth who found Miss Davenport's body."

164

Ada feigned surprise. "Really? I didn't know that."

He leaned across the table and whispered, "And the police think there maybe a connection."

Ada also lowered her voice, not because she'd had a sudden attack of laryngitis, but because she was following his lead. "What do you think it means?" she asked, genuinely interested in his answer. But before he could reply, someone emitted a cough.

Mr Ayres was standing by the table, a slip of paper in his hand. "This message was just telephoned through for you," he said, handing Ada the paper. "I did try your room, but when there was no answer, I thought you might be in here."

Ada read the message and then shoved it into her handbag. "Thank you, Mr Ayres. Very kind of you to come and find me."

"All part of the service," he said in his soft syrupy voice. "I hope you have recovered from your terrible ordeal yesterday."

"I think you'll find it's Miss Katherine who's suffered the terrible ordeal. But, yes, I am quite recovered. As the saying goes, a good night's sleep will cure just about anything."

"I say, Ayres," barked the Major, "have you found this detestable joker yet? Earlier today, I heard someone refer to this place as the Death Bridge Hotel."

Mr Ayres flinched. "Everything is being done to find the culprit. Even the staff - past and present, are being checked again."

Ada raised an eyebrow. "What makes you think it's a member of staff?"

"Because the events suggest it is."

Even though no name had been mentioned, Ada was sure he was referring to Mr Travis. While it was true the valet had been in a prime position to commit the foul deeds, she was equally sure he was not the culprit. So, what game was Ayres playing? Why the subtle accusation?

And then the 'penny' dropped. He was preparing the groundwork for a setup. He was going to lay the blame for all the misdeeds, which included the death of Miss Davenport, at the feet of his ex-employee.

"Speaking of staff," said Ada in a conversational tone, "have you found a replacement for Mr Travis?"

"Travis?" repeated the Major. "What's happened to him?"

If the hotel proprietor intended to answer, Ada did not give him the chance. "He resigned yesterday."

The Major looked surprised. "What on earth for?"

Ada shrugged and spoke as though Mr Ayres was part of the furniture. "No idea. It's such a shame too. Mr Travis was a nice young man. I always enjoyed our chats. It was so refreshing to find a young person who respects the elderly."

Mr Ayres cleared his throat and plastered a smile on his face. "Well, I can't stand here chatting all night. Mrs Harris, would you give me a few minutes of your time this evening? There is something I need to discuss," and without waiting for a reply, he turned and walked away.

The Major shook his head. "You know, in all the years I've been coming here, I've never come to grips with that man. One minute he's as happy as a lark and the next he's as dull as dishwater." He finished his beer and stood up. "Another...erm..." He stared at Ada's drink as though it was something alien. "Lemonade?"

Ada nodded but did not elaborate as to her choice of drink. She waited until he was clear of the table before retrieving the message. It was from Florrie and simply stated, 'Not all records survived the war'.

Florrie had conveyed important information in bland, almost boring terms, and once again Ada posed the question - how much did Florrie know? Indeed, had she really been in ignorance all these years?

"Penny for them," said the Major, returning to the table. He raised his glass of beer. "Cheers."

Ada shoved the message into her handbag again and took a reluctant sip of the lemonade. Perhaps if she really used her imagination, she could change the colour and taste.

"Have you done the crossword tonight?" she asked by way of distraction. For answer, the Major smiled, withdrew the evening paper from his pocket, and flourished it like a baton.

***

The dinner gong had long sounded when the last clue remained unsolved. "Let me read it for myself," said Ada, and turned the paper around. In truth, she was only pretending to be stumped. She wanted to check his handwriting very closely. After a suitable interval she said, "No. I can't get this one."

"Never mind," said the Major, returning the newspaper to his pocket. "We'll get the paper tomorrow and see what the answer was. No doubt we'll kick ourselves when we see it."

***

Dinner was considerably livelier than the night before, and due to the inclement weather, many of the guests were dining in the hotel. Ada and the Major ordered the same meal - pâté, fresh Dover sole with vegetables and sautéed potatoes, and homemade apple pie topped with Cornish cream.

Ada wiped her mouth on a napkin. "They certainly know how to cook here," she said, and then added seamlessly, "was it always like this?"

"Not really, though I suppose it depends on your point of view. Back in the 60's and early 70's, food was pretty stodgy, and the type of meal we've just eaten would have been served in an up-market restaurant. A so-called 'healthy diet' was practically unheard of."

"What sort of food did they serve?"

"Hmm, can't really say off hand. They used to have lamb shanks on the menu but they fell out of favour."

Ada glanced at her watch - it was just after 8.30 pm. As the Inspector was not due for another hour, she had to stall for time. "I don't suppose you have a pack of cards."

"No, but there's probably some in the cocktail lounge. Why?"

"Well, you've been so kind and considerate these past 24 hours, that I thought it was time I bought you a drink, and if you like, play a few games of gin-rummy."

The Major beamed. "Splendid! I accept."

Chapter 17. The Suitcase.

At 9.30 precisely, Inspector Butler entered the cocktail lounge. He obtained an orange juice from the bar and then joined the Major and Ada, who had just claimed 'gin' for the sixth time.

The Major threw down his cards in disgust. "You've missed your vocation, Ada. Oh, good evening, Inspector. What brings you here on such a night?"

Inspector Butler looked pointedly at Ada. "Mrs Harris invited me. I believe she has some information."

Ada took a deep breath. The last thing she wanted was to inflict more pain, but it could not be helped. "Not me, Inspector, but Major Eaton does."

The old soldier looked at her warily. "What do you mean?"

She reached across and patted his hand. "It's alright. You don't have to hide it anymore. You and Mirabelle Davenport were related."

The Major's face turned the colour of grimy white paint. He seemed on the verge of denying the accusation, and then apparently realised that it would be pointless. "How did you know?" he asked.

"It was founded on three principles - age, knowledge, and timing. Miss Davenport told somebody the story of the backstairs just before she died, and that same person repeated it to me earlier today. This then begged the question, how did she know the story?

"The answer, if you think about it, is quite obvious. Only someone who was here at the time would have known. My informant also stated that nobody had ever mentioned the stairs."

"Ah," he replied. "That silly remark I made in the trap about the hotel seeing wartime service."

"Yes. During a dinner party I attended, a psychiatrist said, 'The one subject people enjoy talking about above all others is themselves, and sooner or later they'll reveal something unwittingly'.

"Do you see the point? You weren't born till after the war, and I doubt there are many people still alive who know the name of the military operation. Of course, everyone who has worked here knows about the stairs, but how many would know how they came into being?"

"All those years," he said wistfully, "what a waste. I wish I'd known her. I wonder how long she knew about me before she rang my club."

Ada sighed heavily. "Unfortunately, Major, I suppose that's something you'll never know."

"Excuse me," said the Inspector, "but would one of you tell me what you're talking about?"

"Operation 'Waterloo'," answered the Major. "In early 1945, word filtered down through the Ministry of Defence that several high-ranking German officers wanted to defect. I don't know how they were going to get out of Germany, but suffice to say that once they arrived in England, they had to be kept in a safe place.

"Some Whitehall boffin knew of the hotel and commandeered it. But, there was a problem. There was no route by which the Germans could be smuggled out if necessary, and so a corps of engineers was brought in and built the backstairs.

171

"When the defectors were shot before leaving Germany - no doubt on Hitler's orders, the military packed up and left. Mr Ayres senior never objected to the changes. After all, his hotel had been renovated and it hadn't cost him a penny."

"And Miss Davenport? Where does she fit in?"

The Major stared into his beer as he replied, "My mother and her mother were sisters."

The Inspector looked as if he would explode. "What?"

"I can only remember meeting her once," continued the Major. "I have one photograph of her. Our names are on the back along with a date, 1956, which makes her about twelve and me four.

"My mother later told me that shortly after the photo was taken, Mirabelle and her mother, Elspeth, emigrated to Australia."

Ada held up a finger to interrupt. "Do you know why they left England?"

"No idea, but you can imagine my surprise when, earlier this year, Mirabelle left a message at my club and gave the hotel as her address. We spoke on the phone and naturally we discussed the hotel, during which she told me the story of the backstairs.

"She asked me to join her here as she had, to use her words, 'unearthed something of importance'. She did not elaborate, and being both intrigued and excited to meet her again, I literally caught the next train. But, by the time I arrived, she was dead."

The Inspector looked at him suspiciously. "Why should we believe you? Your entire story could be a complete fabrication. Can you prove your relationship to Miss Davenport?"

Major Eaton scratched his head. "Well, I don't have any birth certificates or anything like that, but I do have the photograph."

Ada felt a squadron of butterflies take flight in her tummy. She accepted that she was too old to be abseiling down buildings or cliffs, or crawling through ancient tunnels, or running the gauntlet of gun toting border guards. Nowadays, her love for her 'second' job was derived from when the epiphysis, or the 'Anagnorisis' as she would have called it, was within her grasp.

She took a deep breath and said, "Major, does anyone else know about the photograph?"

"I don't think so. Is it important?"

Ada was so taken aback by his naivety that she could only reply, "Um...I'm not sure." Is it important indeed! She didn't know whether to kiss or slap him.

She desperately wanted to consult her notes, but she could hardly produce her notebook at the table. An idea came into her head. "If you would excuse me for a few minutes. I must see Mr Ayres before I forget."

***

The proprietor had his back turned and was busy with the pigeonholes. Apart from the presence of the Major, the scene was a repetition of yesterday morning, and Ada was not prepared to be snubbed a second time.

She coughed loudly and said, "You wanted to see me?"

He turned around and for the briefest of seconds, glared at her malevolently. He then pasted a benevolent smile on his face and spoke in his syrupy voice.

"Ah, Mrs Harris. Thank you for coming so promptly. When Miss Katherine informed me that she was leaving tomorrow, it occurred to me that you didn't say how long you would be staying here. Could you give me an indication?"

"Probably until the end of the week. I assume you can accommodate me if I decide to stay longer?"

"I am afraid not," he said with a fake apologetic smile. "We're booked solid for the next few weeks, and after that, I'm not taking any more bookings. The hotel will be closed over the winter for renovations."

Ada returned his fake smile. "I suppose with the redevelopment project, the hotel will need a massive overhaul." She pointedly looked around the foyer. "I have been quite comfortable here, but it definitely needs work. When do you require my room?"

"Well, to be honest, tomorrow. I have two conventions booked in for the weekend, and most of the guests are arriving on Friday."

'This man couldn't lie to save his life' she thought. 'Time for a whopper of my own'. "Unfortunately, if you'll pardon the pun, I cannot accommodate you. My return train ticket is not valid before Friday, so I can't leave until then.

174

"I suppose I could catch an earlier train, but that would incur a penalty, and unless you're prepared to pay it, then I'm afraid you're stuck with me."

Mr Ayres could not have looked at her more contemptuously if he'd tried. "Very well. On Friday, please ensure you vacate the room before 10 o'clock." His expression changed to smugness as he added, "It must be thoroughly cleaned before the new guest takes possession," and seemingly pleased with his inane insult, he turned his back again.

The discussion was over. Ada was so incensed that she forgot about reading her notes. Instead, she twisted her well-worn wedding ring. It was an involuntary gesture that only occurred when she was angry – and she was very angry now. Insults were nothing new to her, but to cast aspersions on her personal hygiene was really hitting below the belt.

"Pretentious upstart," she growled as she stormed into the lounge and resumed her seat.

"What's the matter?" cried the Major, seeing her livid expression.

"You will appreciate this, Major. I have been given my marching orders."

She gave a verbatim account, to which the Major grunted in sympathy. "He said something similar this morning when I enquired about Miss Katherine. He didn't exactly ask me to leave but he may as well have done."

Ada's anger momentarily abated. "Did he now? How very curious."

"Never mind about that," responded the Major, his tone changing to one of excitement. "Listen to

175

this. We were talking while you were gone and..." He broke off and looked at the Inspector. "You tell her. You can explain it better."

"I am satisfied that Major Eaton is who he claims to be, and that he is Miss Davenport's only living relative, though I will still need to see the photograph. This means that I can release her suitcase to him. Actually..."

The Inspector was interrupted by a massive clap of thunder. The lights flickered, the windows rattled, and the paraphernalia hanging from the ceiling swayed like demented seaweed.

"Actually, Mrs Harris," he went on, "it's turned out rather well. After our conversation on the phone, I didn't think you'd be satisfied until you'd examined the suitcase, so I brought it with me. It's in the car."

Ada set her jaw and slapped the table to show she meant business. "Right, gentlemen, drink up, we've got work to do. Major, I want you to get the photograph and search through your belongings for anything that links you to Miss Davenport, no matter how insignificant. Come to my room - number 26, when you've finished. One more thing, do not speak to anyone. I don't care if the Queen walks through the door, ignore her."

"Righty ho." He downed his drink and exited the lounge.

Ada addressed the Inspector. "Please get the suitcase and bring it to my room, and the same applies to you, do not speak to anyone."

But Inspector Butler did not move. Instead, he stroked his chin and looked at her with intense

176

curiosity. "Who are you, Mrs Harris? You're not police and you're not MI5. I checked, or at least, as much as one can check with those secret bods.

"Yet shortly after I made those enquiries, I received a phone call from the Chief Constable himself, who said I was to give you every assistance. He is the real reason why I brought the suitcase."

Ada smiled coyly. "Suffice to say that I'm one of the good guys. Now, shall we go?"

***

A drenched Inspector Butler entered room 26. "Where's the Major?" he asked, laying the suitcase on the bed.

Ada retrieved a towel from the bathroom and handed it to him. "Not here yet," she answered.

The Inspector removed his coat, wiped his face and trousers with the towel, and opened the suitcase. "As I said earlier, not much to show for a lifetime."

Ada gazed avidly at the contents, even though she had no idea what she was looking for. She wanted to examine them without being observed. "Inspector, would you mind checking on the Major? He seems to be taking a long time."

***

No! This is all wrong! I haven't committed three murders for nothing. They won't stop me! Nobody will stop me! Wait...who's that? Ah, come into my parlour said the spider to the fly. Aw...ain't that nice, the door's open. Three murders...do I hear four?

Chapter 18. A Late Night Conference.

Ada made sure the door was locked before setting to work. She scrutinised the toiletries, trinket boxes, some books and magazines, shoes and clothes. She even checked the suitcase itself, but there was nothing of any consequence.

What did strike her as odd however, was the lack of documentation. No letters, no bank or credit card statements, not even a scribbled note. Had she deliberately lived like a hermit, or was this the work of someone else?

Ada stared angrily at the now repacked case, as though willing it to reveal its secret. She was just contemplating a second search when there were two loud bangs on the door. "Who is it?" she called out.

"Butler. Open the door - quick!"

She yanked it open and let out a cry of horror. The Inspector was supporting a dazed Major Eaton, his jacket splattered with blood.

Before Ada could utter a word, Inspector Butler snapped, "Make a cold compress."

Ada ran into the bathroom and soaked towels under the tap. She returned to the room just as the Inspector removed his bloodstained handkerchief from the wound. In light of the nasty gash, the scrap of fabric was akin to mending a broken leg with a band-aid.

"It was all I had to hand," he explained, sounding apologetic. "My primary concern was to get the Major to safety."

Ada applied a towel to the Major's neck. "What happened?" she asked as the cloth turned crimson.

His breathing was short and shallow. "Someone came into my room and clobbered me."

"Did you see who it was?"

"No. I don't know what they wanted, but if it was these..." He reached inside his jacket, and like a magician pulling a rabbit out of a hat, brandished a faded brown envelope. "...photographs!" The moment of exuberance was premature, for he let out a mournful groan.

"Photographs?" queried Ada. "Plural?"

"Yes," he wheezed. "I found another one. I forgot I had it."

"Sit quietly and take deep breaths," said Ada, extracting two small black and white photographs from the envelope.

The first showed a light-haired girl aged about five sitting on a swing. She had large round eyes and a cheeky smile. The second was taken a few years later. Her features were more defined, and beside her was a very young boy with dark hair and a toothy grin.

Ada studied the girl and then looked at the Major. There was definitely a resemblance. She turned the picture over and read, 'Mirabelle and Charlie, July, 1956'.

"Mrs Harris," said Inspector Butler, "please take care of the Major while I go downstairs. I'll be back shortly."

He left the room and Ada continued to apply the compresses. "I think you might need a few stitches. The wound is not wide but it's deep. I wish I had some hot sweet tea or brandy to give you."

The Major tried to chuckle as he extracted a hip flask from a pocket. "Not to worry, my dear, I brought my own. I found it when I was looking for the photo and thought it might come in useful. The irony, eh?

"There's not much in it and I haven't used it in years, so goodness knows what it'll taste like."

"Probably very smooth," she answered, pouring a generous measure into the cup. He tossed it down his throat like a man dying of thirst. She poured a little more, which was all that was left. "Sip this one or you'll probably be sick."

He followed her advice. "The Inspector said you'd sent him to my room. I don't think I am being too dramatic when I say that it saved my life."

Ada was about to respond when there was a soft tap on the door. She looked at the Major, who echoed her 'that's not the Inspector' expression. She moved behind the door and adopted a sleepy voice.

"Who is it?"

"Travis," he whispered.

Ada unlocked the door and he stepped inside. His mouth fell open when he saw the Major. "What..." he began, but was interrupted by yet another knock on the door.

Ada repeated the pantomime and admitted the Inspector, who was carrying a tray of drinks. After placing the glasses of brandy and cups of tea on the dressing table, he turned and faced the ex-valet.

"And who are you?" he asked warily.

Mr Travis removed his cap and unzipped his wet jacket. "Don't you recognise me?"

"Ah, now I do. What are you doing here?"

"I was about to ask him the same thing," said the Major. "Ayres told us earlier that you'd resigned."

"I suggest," said Ada, "that before we start swapping stories, we make ourselves comfortable."

The Inspector sat in the armchair and nursed a glass of brandy. Mr Travis crossed his arms and leaned against the wall, not caring that his soaking jacket was leaving a watermark. The Major, though he eyed the alcoholic restorative, opted for tea instead.

Ada opened the impromptu conference by outlining her ideas and speculation, though she was careful not to overplay her own role in the drama. Everyone listened with rapt attention, the only sound being the rain pelting the windows.

She concluded with, "To paraphrase a friend of mine, what we have here are pieces of disjointed information, rather like a jigsaw puzzle. We have no idea what the finished picture looks like, and unless I'm very much mistaken, Mr Travis is about to add to the puzzle." She smiled at him encouragingly. "Tell us what you discovered this afternoon."

"As I told you this afternoon, Colin Macdonald runs the arcade. However, until recently, he also owned the building and the land." He withdrew several documents from his jacket and read them before continuing, "The whole kit and caboodle was sold about a year ago to a company called Knight Entertainment - that's Knight with a 'K', who are a subsidiary of Breakaway Constructions, registered in the Canary Islands. But Breakaway is also a subsidiary, with the parent company based in London. It's called..." he looked directly at Ada, "...Tomlinson International."

Ada slowly nodded her head. "Well done, Mr Travis."

"You don't seem surprised," commented the Inspector.

"No, I'm not, but to be brutally honest, unlike other adscititious material, I'm not sure where it fits in."

The Inspector raised an eyebrow. "What does...whatever you said, mean?"

"Adscititious - superfluous, irrelevant," she explained, a note of irritation in her voice. Then, realising she'd spoken unfairly, she flashed him an apologetic smile. "I'm not annoyed with you but with myself."

She looked at the suitcase. Why couldn't she put the pieces together? Unconsciously, she put her thoughts into words. "I am absolutely sure the answer to the murders lies in that suitcase, but I'm dashed if I can find it."

The atmosphere in the room was gloomier than a tomb, a situation not helped by the pounding rain and howling wind. In addition, there was a sense of 'well if you can't figure it out, who can?'

Mr Travis fidgeted with the papers in his hand, and having now swapped the tea for brandy, the Major made fine work of holding the glass while applying the compress to his head. Inspector Butler fiddled with the knot of his tie. With four people breathing in a confined space, the room had become rather stuffy.

Ada, who had been absently watching the Inspector, slowly straightened up. The idea, the thought, the suggestion that had eluded her the last time she'd seen Katherine Wilson, had finally blossomed.

Ada was on her feet in an instant. Three pairs of eyes watched as she went to her own suitcase and withdrew the dress she'd worn on Tuesday. She sniffed the fabric and then looked at Mr Travis.

"Please tell me you brought the passkey."

"Yep." He fished it out of his jacket and dangled it between his fingers.

"Good. I want you to go to room 16 and guard Katherine Wilson. I don't care what excuses she makes or how much she rants and raves - sit on her if you have to, but she must not leave that room. Further, nobody is to enter unless it's one of us. Do you understand?"

Mr Travis stared at her. There was no disputing that she was deadly serious, but even so, he hesitated. "Erm...isn't holding someone against their will, illegal?"

Inspector Butler rubbed his nose and spoke in a off-handed tone. "Well, now, that rather depends on your point of view."

When the ex-valet still looked dubious, Ada spoke from the heart. "You have been very brave so far. Please don't let your courage fail now. We need you. We can't catch a killer without your help."

There was a tense silence as everyone looked at him expectantly. He still sounded uncertain as he responded, "Alright. I'll do it."

Ada patted his arm. "Good man. Inspector, you're with me. Major, you stay here and lock the door. Again, do not let anyone in unless it's one of us."

The Major looked disappointed. "Are you sure? Perhaps I could..." but Ada was already shaking her head.

As she picked up her voluminous handbag, the Inspector quipped, "You planning on doing a little shopping while we're out?"

Ada grinned. "A woman's handbag is like an ocean - you never know what secrets lie in its depths." They headed for the door. Ada called back over her shoulder, "Remember, Major, nobody comes into this room."

"Wait," he cried in a jittery voice. "What if the phone rings or someone tries to break in?"

She opened the wardrobe and withdrew the walking stick. "In the case of the former, don't answer it, and in the case of the latter, hit them with this. We'll be back as soon as possible."

Chapter 19. Nocturnal Shenanigans.

Mr Travis unlocked the door to the false room 29. The stairwell was cold and breezy and resonated with disjointed noises. Inspector Butler could not hide his surprise. "Well, I'll be jiggered. I didn't know..." He got no further due to the hand that had suddenly covered his mouth.

"Sorry, Inspector," whispered Mr Travis, his voice so low that it was barely audible. He removed his hand. "I had to shut you up. Sound travels to every floor like a bullhorn."

The Inspector nodded in understanding as he and Ada climbed to the next floor. Room 36 smelt damp and musty, and the only light came from the occasional passing car. "Better close the curtains before turning on the light," advised Ada.

The Inspector did as instructed, and when he turned around, he was astonished to see her standing on the bed. "What on earth are you doing?" he asked.

"Trying to prove a theory," she answered, running her fingers along the topsides of the blades. "I presume your men fingerprinted this room?"

"Thoroughly."

"Did they do up here?"

"Everywhere."

"But they didn't find any prints up here, did they?" It was more a statement than a question.

"No. The blades had been wiped clean."

Ada glanced at her hand. Apart from a thin layer of dust, there was no grime like in the other rooms. "And that, Inspector, is part of the solution. Please pass me my handbag."

Baffled, he duly obliged. Ada extracted the knitting needles she'd bought at the haberdashers, and using the lightest of touches, tried to position them on the fan. She made several attempts but the result was always the same. Due to the curvature of the blades, the needles would not stay in place.

"Perhaps the joker used a bit of sticky tape to keep them in place," he said, helping her to climb down. "Other than that, I'm dashed if I know how it was done."

"That's because it never happened. The scene was crafted to create the illusion that it was a practical joke that went terribly wrong. The blades were cleaned either just before or just after her death. Did you check the blades in some of the other rooms? They are thick with grease and dust - probably never been cleaned since the day they were put up."

The Inspector spoke cautiously. "Are you saying that the flying needle scenario was not the mode of death?"

"Exactly. Do you not see the cleverness? You were influenced by the circumstances. You even told Mr Travis it was the mode of death because there was no other evidence to contradict it, which was exactly what the killer wanted you to think."

For only the second time in his long, distinguished career, Inspector Raymond Butler felt like a chump. He had always taken pride in his capability as a detective, and yet as he stood and watched Ada return the needles to her handbag, his shoulders slumped under the weight of incompetence.

"Do you know how and why Miss Davenport died?"

"Hmm...not exactly but I'm working on it."

The Inspector eyed her speculatively. There was no point chafing over the fact that she was right and he was wrong. Self-recrimination could wait. Right now he wanted answers, and if there was one thing he had learned about her, it was that she played her cards close to her chest.

"You're hiding something," he said bluntly.

"On the contrary. I have the same facts to hand as you do. But I'll tell you this much for nothing, whether she realises it or not, the woman downstairs has another part of the solution."

"Katherine Wilson?" Inspector Butler could not have looked more confused if he'd been told that black was the new white. "What's she got to do with it?" He rubbed his forehead. "Look, Mrs Harris, I'm still trying to work out where Alistair Walsh fits in. That was one heck of a bomb you dropped."

She flashed him a smile. "Patience, Inspector. As they say in the classics, all will be revealed. Now, I need to question Katherine again."

***

Ada straightened the coverlet and switched off the light. They descended the backstairs to room 16, where after identifying themselves, Mr Travis opened the door.

The resentment in the room was almost palpable, and Katherine was instantly on her feet. "What is the meaning of this?" she demanded, glaring at Inspector Butler.

Ada spoke in a harsh, commanding tone. "Sit down!" Unlike their previous meeting, there was no vestige of sympathy. The time for 'niceties' and genteel observances had passed.

"I will not! Get out!"

"Not until you have answered her questions," responded the Inspector, who along with Mr Travis, had taken up a position by the door.

"This is a nightmare! I want to vacate this hotel and never return." She resumed her seat, wrapped her arms around her chest, and rocked back and forth.

Ada sat on the footstool again and began to clap. "Bravo! A fine performance and one worthy of a great actress, but it will avail you nothing...Elizabeth."

There were two sharp intakes of breath behind her, and Ada hoped neither man would interrupt. "Your sister did not commit suicide. She was murdered, and I think I know why. But, only you can prove it."

Elizabeth opened her mouth as if to protest. And then she crumpled like a puppet cut from its strings. Her indomitable personality vanished, leaving a simpering woman behind.

"How did you know it was me?" she asked, tears flowing down her face.

"It was the brooch. Katherine said on Sunday evening that it was the only thing she had belonging to her mother, and that she wore it all the time. And yet you were not wearing it this afternoon nor yesterday.

"Your sister's death was a case of mistaken identity. Nobody except myself knew that you were swapping rooms. I presume you made the exchange on Monday after our walk. Unfortunately, you inadvertently left your bottle of sleeping pills behind, which the killer used to advantage. With no name on the label, the killer had no reason to think that his victim was not you.

"At some point, you realised that the victim should have been you, and as the killer thought you dead, you assumed your sister's identity. You had already exchanged rooms, so why not everything else? Which brings us to the main point - why does someone want you dead?"

Elizabeth wiped her eyes and blew her nose. "I have asked myself that same question a thousand times since she died. In my panic after I found her dead, I forgot to remove the brooch. I swear that I do not know why someone wants me dead."

Ada changed the subject. "Tell me about the days just before Miss Davenport died. I also want to know what happened when you met Alistair Walsh in the haberdashers."

Some of Elizabeth's hauteur returned, in that she spoke evenly and crisply. "There was a distinct change in her personality. The closest description I can apply is that she was euphoric. I believe Travis also observed the change."

They looked at him for confirmation. The ex-valet's cheeks flushed pink. Clearly he did not relish being the centre of attention. "Yes, I did."

Elizabeth continued, "As for Mr Walsh, I don't know that I can shed any light on that. Mirabelle and I were in the haberdashers when he arrived. We were introduced and I departed shortly thereafter."

"Did you hear them speak?" asked Ada.

"Yes. He was very insistent on speaking to her privately. It would have been improper of me to remain in their company, hence why I left the shop and returned to the hotel.

"He did seem extremely pleased to see her, though that could have been due to the weather. It was a particularly hot day, and he was wearing a suit and carrying a briefcase."

Ada heard the Inspector mumble, 'I thought so'. She stored the comment in her memory and then went on, "Did Mr Walsh give any indication as to why he was there?"

The spinster's brow crinkled. "No," she said slowly, "but he did say something that I later thought rather odd. He said, 'During our discussions on the phone, you mentioned that you sometimes came here on a Saturday afternoon'."

Ada leaned forward on the footstool. "Why did that strike you as odd?"

"Because it sounded as if they had never met before, which goes some way to explaining what happened afterwards. I suppose she must have been brooding on the unexpected meeting, because twice during dinner she dropped her knife.

"Later, instead of sitting in the cocktail lounge as usual, she asked me to accompany her to her room. But, when we reached it, she simply said, 'good night' and closed the door."

"Perhaps she just wanted to be alone," commented Ada.

She sighed heavily. The interview was going nowhere, and yet the answer had to be here. She looked at her watch. It was nearly midnight. She thought of the Major waiting anxiously in her room, which suddenly inspired an idea.

"Miss Elizabeth, did Mr Walsh give anything to Miss Davenport? A book, an envelope, a photograph?"

Elizabeth opened her mouth, and Ada was sure she was going to say 'no. And then the spinster dropped her head and could not have looked more ashamed. "Not that I am aware of, but later that day, Mirabelle gave something to me. I know I should have mentioned it earlier, but I did not want to be accused of theft. Besides, I didn't see what difference it would make."

Try as she might, Ada could not summon any empathy. While she understood the desperate act of subterfuge - and goodness knew how many times she'd employed it herself in the past, there was something about Elizabeth's attitude that conveyed a lack of sincerity.

Had she said something like, 'Oh dear, how sad, pass the cucumber sandwiches', it would have exemplified her character perfectly. Moreover, the only reason she had cried was because she'd been caught. Ada was disgusted by the woman's selfishness, and was glad when the Inspector spoke up.

"The truth," he said sternly, "no matter how painful, is always the best. Just, tell us what happened."

"Before Mirabelle said 'goodnight' to me for what proved to be the last time, she gave me a small box and told me to take it to my room. She said, 'I have just received this and I think you'll find the contents very interesting'."

"Did she receive it from Mr Walsh?"

"I don't know. She didn't say. I put the box in my room and went downstairs to join Katherine. It was only when I retired for the night that I remembered the box, but by then the hour was too late to return it. As it transpired, it was too late in every respect."

"Who knew you had the box?"

"Nobody. I kept it out of sentiment."

"And what did it look like?"

Elizabeth looked confused, as though she'd been asked to describe the colour red to a blind person. "But, you've seen it. It was the jewellery box."

Inspector Butler let out a groan of despair, and Ada slumped back on the stool. Had she literally held the answer in her hands? "Where is it now?" she asked.

Elizabeth pointed to the nightstand. Ada retrieved the box. Everything looked the same. "You said yesterday that this was your sister's jewellery."

Elizabeth dropped her head again. "I also lied about that. I know you must think me a very wicked woman, but I did not want anyone to know of its existence - not even Katherine."

"But how did it end up in her room?"

"It was not her room. It was mine. If you recall, we did not exchange rooms till Monday afternoon. Yesterday, somehow through my grief, I realised I'd left it behind and just had to get it back. It was a part of Mirabelle that I could cherish forever, and the last thing I wanted was for it to go missing."

If there had been anything breakable to hand, such as a lamp with a hideous brown base, it probably wouldn't have survived. Never had Ada's epithet of 'silly old fool' been more apt. Unlike Mrs Osborne, who had abstained from telling the police what she knew because of hurt pride, Elizabeth's motive had been pure selfishness, underpinned by arrogance and conceit.

Inspector Butler stepped forward and spoke in a barely controlled voice. "You realise that your information sheds new light on Miss Davenport's death, and more than likely, Alistair Walsh as well."

"And quite possibly," said Ada tonelessly, "that of your sister."

The colour steadily drained from Elizabeth's face. "You…you think there's a connection?"

Ada was faced with a dilemma. On the one hand, she did not want to frighten the foolish woman by answering in the affirmative, but on the other hand, there was no guaranteeing she was safe in the hotel. Erring on the side of caution, Ada made a suggestion.

"Inspector, I think Elizabeth and Major Eaton should leave the hotel at once."

Elizabeth jumped to her feet, her expression furious. "The Major? What has he to do with it? He is responsible for all the practical jokes!"

Ada hoped she was not acting prematurely when she stood up and 'squared off'. "No, he is not. I don't know where you got that idea from, but to the best of my knowledge, Major Eaton has never harmed anyone in his life. You have been vilifying the wrong man and treating him most cruelly."

During his time in 'the met', Inspector Butler had seen many women fight like alley cats, but most had been under the age of forty. There was something distasteful about two elderly matrons standing toe-to-toe, and he thought it prudent to intervene.

"You think Miss Elizabeth and the Major are in danger?"

Ada turned away. She could hardly bear to look at the spinster. It was tempting to leave her to face the consequences of her actions, but that would also mean abandoning the Major, and that was something Ada was not prepared to do. Whether she liked it or not, they must both be given protection.

"They have a strong connection to Miss Davenport, and I believe she's at the heart of it all. I strongly urge you to get them away at least until tomorrow." When the Inspector nodded in ascent, Ada turned back to the spinster. "Take only what you need for a day or two. Everything else can wait."

***

Ada kept a tight hold on the jewellery box as they filed into her room. Elizabeth shrieked when she saw the Major and his bloody clothes. He reassured her that it looked worse than it was, and that all he had was a thumping headache. Surprisingly, she offered to try and clean his jacket.

"There's no time," said Ada, and explained the situation to the Major. Shortly thereafter, Mr Travis led everyone except Ada, down the backstairs and through the kitchen.

The howling wind and driving rain were unforgiving. Urgent necessity aside, only someone with a death wish or a weird obsession for storms would be out on such a night. Unfortunately, the Inspector and his charges had no choice but to brave the elements. Nor did Elizabeth object when each man took an arm and hurried her down the street to the Inspector's car.

Mr Travis watched the car drive away, the red brake lights shining like demonic eyes in the darkness. He re-entered the kitchen, raided a refrigerator and a cupboard, and returned to room 26.

"I don't know about you," he said, placing the purloined goods on the dresser, "but all this excitement has made me hungry."

Ada stared at the impromptu feast. "But, won't it be missed?" she asked, somewhat alarmed. The last thing she needed was the theft to be discovered, though she was secretly pleased to see that he'd snaffled her favourite biscuits – custard creams.

Mr Travis had no such qualms. "Are you kidding? There's enough food down there to feed a third world country. I'm just sorry it's not a more dignified spread."

Ada poured out two glasses of milk. "It was very kind of you," she said sincerely, opening the packet of biscuits.

There was a short silence while they ate their fill. "So," he asked, brushing crumbs from his trousers, "what do we do next?"

"I don't think anything else will happen tonight. As for tomorrow, that's another matter."

Mr Travis glanced at his watch. "You mean today," he corrected.

Ada looked at her travelling alarm clock. It was nearly 1 am. "Goodness me, so it is. Where did the time go?"

"Speaking of time, what time do you want me to return in the morning?"

Ada smiled and pointed to the chair. "I think it would be better if you stayed here. There's a spare pillow and blankets in the wardrobe."

Mr Travis laughed and rattled the passkey. "And I know where there's more if I need them."

The key reminded Ada of what Mr Ayres had said earlier, and when she finished explaining, the ex-valets face changed from healthy pink to feverish red. "You mean the bastard was planning to set me up?"

"It sounded that way to me. I don't think he would have succeeded, but he would certainly have cast doubt on your honesty."

Mr Travis removed his jacket and opened the wardrobe door. "You wait," he said angrily, extracting the pillow and blanket, "I'll get even with that creep if it's the last thing I do."

Chapter 20. The Real Mr Ayres.

It was nearly seven o'clock when Ada and her 'roomy' stood behind the door. "Good luck, Mr Travis, and whatever you do, don't fall asleep." It was not a rebuke, and nor was it a reminder of when he'd inadvertently overslept. It was a simple statement of fact.

"I won't - I promise. Oh, by the way…"

"Yes?" she said quickly, her voice betraying her apprehension.

The ex-valet looked into her eyes. Should he tell her? The plan they had hatched before going to sleep required intense concentration, so perhaps now was not the best time to mention it.

"Never mind. It can wait," and giving her a smile of confidence, he stepped into the corridor.

Ada closed the door and then began cleaning the room, throwing crumbs and empty packets out of the window. She then removed the brown velvet box from under her pillow. In the faint hope that it would sub-consciously provide inspiration, she had literally and figuratively, slept on it. But the box had remained stubbornly silent, and the glue, the reason, the thread that linked everything together, was as elusive now as it was at the start.

She brushed the top with her fingers. "What is it about you that has caused the death of three people?" she murmured, and tipped the contents onto the bed.

Each piece was examined very carefully. Even the backs of the watches - broken and otherwise, were inspected. But, there was nothing out of the ordinary. More out of exasperation than hope, she picked up the now empty box and shook it. Something rattled.

It took her but a moment to expose the object. Hidden in a cavity in the base of the box was an old and much folded piece of paper.

With slightly trembling hands, she read the document and then closed her eyes. She took deep steadying breaths, and for the first time in days, felt her shoulders relax. This was it. This was the answer. She now knew everything…well, almost.

Intuition and common sense had been her guiding forces for over forty years, and if she was to set a trap with herself as bait, then she must employ her instincts as never before. First however, she needed to take a walk.

Ada returned the jewellery to the box and placed it in the bedside drawer. It didn't matter now how many times her room was searched. The evidence was hidden in the most unlikely of places. She donned her hat and coat, picked up her handbag, and went downstairs.

Mr Ayres was busy behind the reception desk, his pasty face frazzled and pink. It seemed a group of guests had suddenly found they needed to be somewhere else. Not bothering to leave her key, Ada exited the hotel.

There were few signs of the torrential storm, and the sun was playing hide and seek behind billowy clouds. On the beach, seagulls fossicked in the detritus that had washed ashore. Ada hurried to the phone box and dialled a London number.

"Yes, that's what I said, 1956 or thereabouts. Within the hour...everything...ring the hotel and insist on speaking to me. Remember Switzerland 1978? Well, its that sort of situation.

"Oh, don't fuss, Bert. You know I never carry a gun. I couldn't hit the side of a barn. I'll probably be in the dining room when you call. Just wish me luck and for God's sake be careful what you say."

Ada exited the box. She knew Bert would move heaven and earth to obtain the decade's old information. The problem was the timing. In order for the plan to work, it had to be executed with the preciseness of a Swiss watch.

Trying not to think of the pending event, Ada strolled along the foreshore and took in lungfulls of salty air. She saw a large piece of driftwood lying on the sand. It reminded her of the pier. Was it still standing? If she got the chance, she would go down and take a look.

By association, she thought of Katherine Wilson. Could her death have been prevented? Had she, Ada Harris, failed?

Ada suddenly felt very old, and her family in Australia very far away. She gazed at the horizon and remembered Semaphore jetty in Adelaide, with its quaint shops, outdoor cafes, and the ice-cream parlour that boasted over 200 flavours.

It had been several years since she'd gone 'down under', so perhaps it was time to consider the dreaded R word – retirement. Yet as she stood contemplating her future, she could not get the image of the giggling Katherine Wilson and the book she would never write, out of her head.

"Not yet," she whispered defiantly. "Not until I've caught her killer," and with renewed vigour and determination she returned to the hotel.

***

Mr Ayres looked at Ada as if she'd suddenly grown two heads. "I beg your pardon?"

Ada was the epitome of cool. She was in no mood to pander or compromise. "Did you not hear me? I said there has been a change in my plan and I will not be leaving until Sunday."

Mr Ayres almost choked as he began to object. "Mrs Harris, I don't think…"

"Also," she went on, ignoring his protest, "I'm expecting a very important call within the hour. Do not take a message. I will either be at breakfast or in my room – good morning."

The proprietor's face turned a sickly shade of puce as Ada entered the dining room. Sitting at her usual table, she had a sudden attack of melancholy. She had become so accustomed to the Major's company, that not to see him seated opposite was akin to losing a dear friend.

"Snap out of it," she quietly rebuked. "This is not the time for sentiment."

***

Ada had almost finished her breakfast when Mr Ayres appeared by the table. He sat down without invitation, and his tone was so outrageously sweet that it was a wonder he wasn't spitting sugar cubes.

202

"Mrs Harris, I am terribly sorry but I cannot offer you further accommodation. As I explained to you last night, the hotel is fully booked for the weekend. You will have to checkout tomorrow as planned," and giving her a fake sympathetic smile, he stood up and began to leave.

"I don't think so," she said acidly.

He stopped, the smile fading from his face. "I beg your pardon?"

"Do you really think I swallowed that bilge last night? You're not renovating the hotel - you're selling it. How do I know this? Simple, because in these days of economic uncertainty, any competent proprietor would be inviting his guests to return. But, instead of encouraging future business, you've done everything to repel it.

"As for the weekend, well in case you hadn't noticed, two of your guests are missing."

Looking as if he was about to faint, Mr Ayres groped for the chair and slowly resumed his seat. "Two of my guests are what?" he said, his voice both incredulous and nervous. "Would you mind telling me what you're talking about?"

Ada raised her cup of tea. A moment later, the contents were spreading across the table. "Oh! How clumsy of me!" She stood inert, as if stunned by what she'd done. In reality, she watched in satisfaction as a stream of the beverage ran off the table and fell in his lap.

Ayres jumped to his feet, flapping his trousers as if trying to take flight. He only had himself to blame, for it was he who had given her the idea. If he could fake sincerity, then why couldn't she?

Moreover, it was a delaying tactic until Bert rang the hotel. It would also annoy the proprietor even further, which was precisely what Ada wanted.

She made a great fuss of mopping up the tea, then, grabbing another napkin, offered to wipe his trousers. "Did it scald you?" she enquired, her concern literally skin-deep.

"Never mind about that," he growled. "I want to know what you meant about two missing guests."

"Major Eaton has taken Katherine Wilson away. I spoke to her just before they left, and she told me that the Major knows a nice quiet out-of-the-way place where she can mourn in peace. So, she won't be going to Wales as planned."

Mr Ayres tugged at his collar as though it were strangling him. "Did they leave a forwarding address? Miss Wilson and I had made arrangements that I would send her luggage to her. What am I supposed to do with it now? And what about their bills? I swear I'll put the police onto them if they don't pay up."

Ada was superb as she responded, "Calm down, Mr Ayres. Miss Katherine and the Major have only taken the things they want, the remainder is to be given to charity. As for their bills, I have two signed blank cheques in my bag. So, you see, those problems are solved.

"As my room is booked for the weekend, I'll have one of theirs instead." She paused for dramatic effect. "Which reminds me, Miss Katherine gave me a present to say thank you for helping her. Even in the midst of her grief she thought of me. It was really nice of her to show her appreciation, even though I did little to deserve it."

Mr Ayres stood up so violently that his chair toppled over. "Charity…cheques…present?" he stammered, his eyes almost popping out. He looked quite mad. He started to walk away but once again Ada stopped him.

"You won't forget about my phone call, will you?"

"No," he answered through gritted teeth, and with his hands shaking with rage, he stormed out of the room.

There was an outbreak of murmuring, and heads swivelled between the now empty doorway and Ada. Completely unconcerned, she went to the buffet and obtained a fresh pot of tea. She checked her watch as she returned to the table. It was nearly nine o'clock.

"Come on, Bert," she said under her breath, "I'm a sitting target here."

She sipped her tea and thought of Miss Davenport. Had she also been a sitting target? If so, then not only would it explain her pendulous moods on the last day of her life, but the reason why she had asked Elizabeth Wilson to escort her to her room.

Ada suddenly leaned forward. Another thought had just flashed into her mind. "Now, I wonder," she murmured, and turning her head, stared sightlessly out of the window.

***

The staff cleared the remnants of breakfast, and it was the sound of the chinking dishes that brought Ada out of her reverie. She exited the dining room and went to the lift, and although she had the expression of someone without a care in the world, her eyes were watching everything around her.

She reached the second floor just as Inspector Butler entered the hotel. He was greeted by a smiling Mr Ayres, who now seemed restored to equanimity. The Inspector went to the lift, and seeing that it was now on the third floor, took the stairs instead.

Ada unlocked her door and stepped inside. The gasp she emitted upon seeing the ransacked room was short lived. An arm shot out of nowhere and wrapped around her neck.

Her own arms flailed like psychotic windmills, causing her handbag to sail across the room and hit the window. "Florrie," she choked, but to the man squeezing the life out of her, it sounded like 'sorry'.

"Ha! Too late for sorry! Where is it? I know you've got it! She gave it to you. Tell me where it is or your death will be slow and painful."

Suddenly, she was propelled across the room with such force, that nothing but a safety net could have stopped her. She crashed to the floor on her injured right hip, her head barely missing the dressing table.

Shaking and winded, she managed to shuffle around and look towards the door. The ex-valet was sitting on a prostrate Mr Ayres, one arm bent high up his back.

"Are you alright?" asked Mr Travis, looking very pleased with himself.

Though still shaken, Ada used the remains of the slashed bed to pull herself up. "Yes," she said hoarsely, rubbing her aching neck.

"Sorry I had to push so hard, but it was the only way to stop this creep."

"And I have another way," said Ada angrily. She found what was left of her dressing gown and removed the belt. She gave it to Mr Travis, who did not need instructions.

Inspector Butler appeared in the doorway. He looked at the prostrate man and then at Ada. "Would you mind explaining why you have Mr Ayres trussed up like a chicken?" He suddenly stopped, his face a picture of confusion. "Wait a moment. This isn't possible. I just saw him at the reception desk."

Still caressing her swollen neck, Ada announced, "No, Inspector, you saw one Mr Ayres, now meet the second."

The Inspector gaped at the man on the floor. And then the 'penny' dropped. "Identical twins?" he posed incredulously.

"Yes."

He reached into his raincoat and pulled out a police radio. He issued a set of instructions and then assisted Mr Travis in placing Mr Ayres into the armchair. Ignoring her throbbing hip, the beat of which not even a troop of samba dancers could have matched, Ada bent over and removed a piece of tissue paper from her shoe.

"Is this what you were after?" she asked, peeling back the tissue and exposing a document.

Inspector Butler eyed the piece of paper. "What is it?" he asked.

"The answer to everything." She gave it to him. "Be careful when you unfold it. It's quite fragile."

"No!" Mr Ayres struggled against his bonds, his eyes filled with murderous intent. "That's private property! It's not yours! Give it back and release me immediately!"

In a rare lapse of control, Ada expressed her feelings. "You are quite correct, Mr Ayres, it is most certainly private property, but it's not yours. You and your contemptible brother murdered three people for it, and I'll be damned before I give it to you."

"Shut up you old hag!" He turned frenzied eyes on Inspector Butler. "She is mad! Are you just going to stand there and listen to the ravings of a lunatic? If you don't do something, I'll sue the police for every penny they've got!"

He started to rise and would have made a dash for the door had Mr Travis not let forth a right hook. Though the blow didn't knock the proprietor out, it did have the effect of stopping him. Cedric Ayres fell back in the chair and whimpered like a baby.

Mr Travis 'danced' like a boxer, fist curled and ready to fly. "You murdering slimy creep. I should hit you again for trying to set me up."

"No, don't do that," said the Inspector with a grin. "I would have to arrest you for assault and he's not worth the paperwork."

Just then, his radio crackled to life. "We got him, sir. He was trying to sneak out through the kitchen."

"Where is he?"

"We put him in the cocktail lounge. Seems the only drink he wants is his brother's blood."

***

They trooped downstairs, Inspector Butler keeping a firm grip on the still simpering Cedric Ayres. The switchboard was buzzing like a hornet, and more from decency than loyalty, Mr Travis went behind the reception desk and began answering the calls.

Ada was about to walk down the dimly lit corridor when he yelled out, "Mrs Harris! Phone! Where do you want to take it?"

Meanwhile in the cocktail lounge, two uniformed officers were guarding a second Mr Ayres. As soon as the brothers clapped eyes on each other, the blame game began, the tirade of accusations degenerating into violent abuse.

Three more officers joined the party, including Sergeant Briggs. He saw the pink, makeshift handcuffs and looked at the Inspector bemusedly.

"A belt? Is this a gentler approach to policing or are you going soft in your old age?"

"Less of your cheek, lad."

The belt was swiftly replaced with proper handcuffs. "Sergeant, escort these guests to our hotel - separate rooms of course."

Ada entered the lounge just as the brothers were being taken away, their continuing heated exchange reminding her of two spitting cobras. She was about to speak to the Inspector when somebody spoke from behind.

"Caught yourself a couple of killers, eh?" Ada spun around. Major Eaton was standing in the doorway, a smiling Miss Elizabeth by his side. "You took a hell of a risk, old girl," he went on, his face beaming in admiration. "You could have been killed."

Mr Travis popped his head around the corner and grinned like a Cheshire cat. He knew exactly what to do. He returned to the desk and effectively took the phone off the hook. He then went to the kitchen and spoke to the staff, at the same time making a special request.

Chapter 21. The First Explanation.

Should anyone have looked through the picture window, they would have been forgiven for thinking that the tableaux was a meeting of a book club or similar. The Inspector, the Major, the ex-valet, and the spinster, all sat round a table, their eyes focused on Ada.

"Before I begin," she said, "there are two points you must bear in mind. Firstly, there were events which none of us were witness too, thereby causing gaps in the chain of events. I will attempt to bridge these gaps based on the balance of probability.

"Secondly, there are questions that are yet to be asked, the answers of which may cause considerable variation to the events. I should also point out that, due to the passage of time, some questions will never be answered. Do you understand?"

Four heads nodded at once. She had their complete attention. "Good. Now, in short, this is what I think happened, but my interpretation is open to speculation.

"In simple terms, three separate events became entwined." She counted them off on her fingers. "The practical jokes, and the deaths of Miss Davenport and Alistair Walsh.

"Our story begins in 1944 when William Frederick Ayres married Elspeth Davenport. A year later he established the hotel. That same year, Elspeth gave birth to a daughter - Mirabelle. I suppose I should call her by her rightful surname of Ayres, but as we are accustomed to Davenport, I'll stick with that.

211

"We now jump forward to 1956, where in the intervening years, two young boys - Cedric and Herbert, had come to live at the hotel. Perhaps William Ayres initially claimed that they were orphans of the war, but in any event, Elspeth found out that they were her husband's illegitimate sons.

"Unfortunately, the stigma of being 'born on the wrong side of the blanket' was still in full effect, and probably to escape the shame and scandal, Elspeth and her daughter went to the other side of the world."

"Good God!" cried the Major. "How on earth do you know that?"

"You told me." Ada delved into her handbag, withdrew her notebook, and flicked through the pages. "In the trap on Tuesday you said, 'I missed her terribly when she and her daughter suddenly emigrated to Australia', and the date on the back of the photo is 1956."

"What photo?" asked Elizabeth.

The Major handed it over just as a middle-aged woman in a purple dustcoat, her expression one of intense curiosity, wheeled a tea trolley with cakes and sandwiches into the room. She went to pick up a large silver teapot, but was halted by Elizabeth's imperious command.

"That will do. I shall pour. We will call if anything is required."

The woman could not have looked more disappointed, and with the corners of her mouth turned down, she bustled out of the room. To Ada's surprise, Elizabeth looked at her and gave her an exaggerated wink.

The tea was poured, and Ada waited until the spinster had finished playing mother before speaking again. "Before I resume the chain of events, I must diverse slightly. Even though the boys were identical twins, there were two distinct differences, the first being their personalities. For the present, I will simply say that one was good and the other evil. The second difference I will leave till later.

"Now we jump to 1969 when Mirabelle returned to England. Regrettably, nobody knows what happened to her afterwards, unless you, Miss Elizabeth, can recall anything she said in this regard. In fact, if you remember anything at all, please speak up."

With genteel graciousness, Miss Elizabeth slowly inclined her head. Inspector Butler, however, was not so courteous. "How do you know she returned in 1969?"

Ada had no intention of revealing that this was part of the information Bert had imparted a short time earlier. "Public records and the Internet," she said airily, as though this explained it. She went on before he could question her further. "The next fact we know for certain is that Miss Davenport came here about four months ago. The obvious question is - why?

"There are any number of reasons, but my own theory is that, being in the twilight of her years, she wanted to spend the remainder of her life in peace and relative comfort. She remembers a time when life was much simpler and her mother still alive, and decides to return to her former home.

"Now, approximately 18 months earlier, Breakaway Constructions had won the right to redevelop the town. Property owners were persuaded to sell, and those who refused were subject to a council compulsory purchase order. The obvious question here is, did Miss Davenport know about the redevelopment before she arrived here?"

Ada paused to give any of them an opportunity to reply or make a comment. When nobody spoke up she went on, "In my opinion, she did not know about the redevelopment. However, I do believe that when she returned to the hotel, she recognised her half-brothers, even though it had been years since she'd seen them.

"From what I learned of her character, I don't think she was particularly stupid or senile. Therefore, it would not have taken her long to ascertain that her father was dead, and that as a consequence, she had a claim to the hotel.

"It would take some time to establish if her father made a Will, so in the interim, she simply enjoyed her life here and the company of her new friends. What she did not know however, was that about two months earlier, a deal had been struck between the brothers and Breakaway Constructions.

"But, there was a problem. Breakaway would only pay the asking price if the hotel was vacant. Being in a prime location, they didn't want it as a going concern, they wanted the land."

Elizabeth politely raised a finger to interrupt. "And that's when the practical jokes began." It was half-question, half-statement.

"Yes," replied Ada. "The brothers needed to 'persuade' the long-term residents to leave, and so began a campaign to make their life here very uncomfortable. But then a second and potentially more dangerous problem emerged. Miss Davenport recognised their 'modus operandi'. Perhaps they played the same tricks when they were children.

"The important point here, is that the brothers knew what she, as yet, did not, namely, that their father had left his estate to be divided equally amongst his children."

Inspector Butler clicked his fingers, as though his mental 'light bulb' had just switched on. "Ah, so that's where Alistair Walsh fits in. No wonder he dragged himself down here. Her claim was worth millions."

Ada was glad his 'policeman's' brain was catching up. It would save awkward questions later. "I think it's safe to assume that he conveyed the news to her before he arrived here. Remember, Elizabeth and Mr Travis both stated that she was very happy in the days before she died.

"Which brings us to the nitty gritty. In order to establish her claim, she would need proof of her parentage. Now, no doubt when the brothers put the pieces together, they frequently searched her room for any relevant documents. But, they never found any. Why? Because Alistair Walsh had them.

"She was also a threat on another front. Everyone was accustomed to seeing a single Mr Ayres, whereas Miss Davenport knew differently. I was guilty of the same mistake myself."

"So, what tipped you off?" asked the Inspector.

Ada took a sip of her now cool tea before replying, "Several things. Firstly, in every room there is a hotel brochure, and realistically, very few people bother to read it. Yet on the inside front cover there is a short history of the hotel, and it clearly states 'sons'.

"Secondly, the Major made several remarks, which on their own didn't mean much. His first comment was about being in two places at once, and then he said, 'his moods swing like a monkey through the trees'.

"Although its now academic, he said last night, 'one minute he's as happy as a lark and the next he's as dull as dishwater'. In addition, not only was my room being searched but I was being watched." She shrugged. "It all began to add up."

There was an awkward silence in which Mr Travis lowered his eyes and inspected his shoes, Major Eaton stroked his moustache, Inspector Butler sat somewhat stunned, and Elizabeth Wilson gaped open-mouthed.

"The brothers made fools of us all," said the spinster, summing up the collective mood. "Sometimes the blatantly obvious is too blatant to be obvious."

"Very true," agreed Ada. "Now, let us turn our attention to what would prove to be her last day alive. She meets Alistair Walsh in the haberdashers. Nobody saw her return to the hotel.

"After dinner, she asked Elizabeth to escort her to her room, at which point she gives her a jewellery box and says, 'I have just received this and I think you'll find the contents very interesting'."

"The Major sat bolt upright. "Walsh gave it to her!"

"Oh, undoubtedly, but why did she give it to Elizabeth?"

"I wish I knew," commented the lady in question.

"Unfortunately," said Ada, "the answer to that is as tragic as it is simple. The box contained a hidden document - a birth certificate to be exact, and as a friend of mine recently commented, 'not all records survived the war'.

Inspector Butler frowned. "You mean there's no copy?"

"Yes, and somehow the brother's found out. Perhaps they taunted her about her claim, calling her an impostor or something like that. It would be perfectly natural that she would want to prove them wrong, and I think that when she returned from seeing Alistair Walsh, she showed them the certificate.

"They probably threatened her or called the document a forgery. Either way, she now feared for her safety, which is why she gave the box to Elizabeth."

"And why she asked me to escort her to her room," remarked the spinster.

"Yes. Later that night, the brothers, either singularly or together, paid her a visit. No doubt they'll claim that they only intended to intimidate her into dropping her claim. In any event, whether it was from a heart attack or an external source, she died.

"As far as the brothers were concerned, her death was the answer to their prayers. All they had to do was cover their tracks, so they concocted two false trails for the police to follow.

"The first was the flying knitting needle scenario. It was a supposed practical joke that went horribly wrong. The damnable thing is, the spate of jokes can be corroborated by past or present guests.

"The second trail was her knitting bag. By disposing of it outside the hotel in a place where it was sure to be found, it suggested that Miss Davenport had been killed by an intruder.

There were tears in Elizabeth's eyes as she said, "Please tell me the truth. Was my sister killed because I had the box?"

Ada gently squeezed the elderly spinster's hand. "Yes. As I said to you last night, your sister was killed by mistake. You must have been terrified when you realised that you were the intended victim, hence why you tried to pass yourself off as your sister. But, like me at the time, you did not know the reason why she died.

"I think it's safe to say that, because the brothers couldn't find the document and you were Miss Davenport's closest friend, they naturally assumed you had it. Remember, apart from myself, nobody knew you were swapping rooms. Consequently, they entered the wrong room."

Inspector Butler said, "What would have happened if Miss Davenport had not revealed her identity? No half sister, ergo, no claim."

"Assuming she did not reveal that she knew who was behind the practical jokes, then she would

218

still be alive. Being cruel selfish creatures, the objective of the brothers to force the long-term residents to leave, never wavered.

"However, I would add a caveat to that. The brothers' may claim that they didn't know who she was, and that her death was the result of a copycat joker. Now, if they can convince a jury of that, then I'm afraid, Inspector, you'll have to start again."

Mr Travis looked puzzled. "I'm sorry, Mrs Harris, but I don't follow you."

It was the Major who answered. "At the moment, the only evidence against the brothers in regard to my cousin is circumstantial. You and Miss Elizabeth are the only people who can testify that Mirabelle was happier than usual before she died. Now, if it wasn't the prospect of an inheritance claim that caused the change, then what did? What motive did the brothers have for killing her?"

The ex-valet was outraged. "You mean they could get away with it?"

"Not if I can help it," replied the Inspector robustly. "Plenty of murderers have been convicted on circumstantial evidence." He turned to Ada. "Would you mind satisfying my curiosity on two points?"

"If I can. I don't have all the answers."

"Firstly, you said earlier that there were two distinct differences between the brothers. You have already explained one, but what is the other? Secondly, what sparked your interest in the matter?"

Ada extracted the vile note from her voluminous handbag. "I believe both questions can be answered with this."

219

The Major read it first. "Disgraceful," he said, and handed it to the Inspector, who after reading it, made no comment and passed it to Mr Travis.

"This is the product of a sick mind," he said, holding the note out to Miss Elizabeth, who did not take it.

"Would you mind reading it allowed? In my hasty departure last night, I forgot to put my reading glasses in my handbag."

Mr Travis cleared his throat. "'The whores of Babylon, the sluts of Whitechapel, the harlots of Jericho, the harridans of China. All these are you and more, Mrs Harris'."

"I received it the day after I arrived," said Ada.

The Inspector looked slightly confused. "But how does it answer my first question?"

"Well, I admit it's more a guess, but I'm sure if you check the registration book behind the reception desk, you'll find two different styles of handwriting."

"That was very observant of you," said Elizabeth.

"More than me," said Mr Travis dolefully. "I worked here for almost a year and didn't notice there were two of them."

Ada returned the note to her handbag. She needed it for her report. "Don't be too hard on yourself. The brothers had everyone fooled. If it's of any comfort to you, they made two mistakes yesterday, though the first is more a question of timing.

"When I opened the door to admit the Inspector into Elizabeth's room, I saw Ayres standing in the

220

passageway. And yet the Inspector stated that Ayres was downstairs with Katherine's body.

"The second mistake has more substance. Last night when Ayres asked me to attend the reception desk, he claimed I had not told him how long I wished to stay. Not only did I tell him five days when I rang up and booked a room, but it was mentioned when I arrived and filled out the registration card."

Elizabeth seemed to hesitate before asking, "To borrow from the Inspector, if Miss Davenport had not revealed her identity nor made any mention of a claim, would my sister still be alive?"

Ada looked at her teacup and wished it would change into something else - like a glass of whiskey. She did not like breaking bad or distressing news.

"Yes," she answered simply.

Inspector Butler stood up and flexed the tiredness out of his shoulders. "Well, if you will excuse me, I have a great deal of work to do. No doubt I will speak to all of you again in due time."

The Major stood up to shake hands, and then suddenly slumped back in his chair, his face ashen. Everyone made overtures of concern but he quickly waved them aside. Nevertheless, he produced a handkerchief and mopped his brow.

"I've just had a thought," he said, "the repercussions of which are extraordinary." He looked at the Inspector. "Would I be correct in assuming that, as Mirabelle's only direct relative, her share of the hotel is now…mine?"

221

Clearly this prospect had not occurred to anyone, for Ada and Elizabeth gaped at the Major, while Mr Travis, his ears literally twitching in anticipation, sat on the edge of his seat.

Inspector Butler seemed to take a long time before replying, "It is illegal to profit from the proceeds of a crime, and that was certainly the intention of the brothers. So, in my opinion, the answer is 'yes'."

It was Elizabeth who drove the reality home. "I think I will go and lie down for a while. It's been a hectic 24 hours. I presume I can still use the room, Major?"

In what can only be considered a supreme act of forgiveness, he took her hand and like a chivalrous knight, kissed the back of it. "Of course you can. As far as I am concerned, you can stay in the hotel as long as you like - no charge."

Elizabeth blushed as she left the room. Mr Travis was similarly affected. Rather than a man in his early 20's, he looked more like a schoolboy as he bounded over to the Major and vigorously shook his hand.

"You're the boss now. I don't suppose you have a job for an ex-valet?"

This time it was the Major who was embarrassed. "Well…erm…" He glanced at Ada for guidance, who subtly jerked her head towards the foyer. He caught her meaning. "I know nothing about running a hotel, and until matters are settled, it'll need a firm hand on the tiller - pardon the pun. I don't suppose you know of anyone who might be interested?"

Mr Travis could hardly contain his excitement as he stepped forward and embraced Ada. "By the way, my name is Travis Smith, not Mr Travis. That's what I was going to tell you this morning when we were standing behind the door to your room," and still grinning like a schoolboy left the lounge.

Ada poured the last of the tea from the pot. It was barely warm but she didn't care. The killings and the jokes were over, and somehow the hotel seemed lighter for it.

She looked out of the window. The clouds had blown away, exposing a tempting if watery sun. Could she be a glutton and return to the fish & chip shop? She sighed. No. Her work was done. It was time to go home.

Chapter 22. The Second Explanation.

Unlike Katherine Wilson, Mrs Harris had never thought of writing a book about her adventures. If she did, then the authorities might be tempted to reactivate the dungeons in the Tower of London. Moreover, if certain items in her lounge room could talk, the ramifications would last for years.

The scimitars above the door had been given to Frank Harris after he had saved an influential, middle-eastern diplomat from being 'quietly' beheaded. Similarly, the American Indian headdress on the chimneybreast was in gratitude for stopping an unscrupulous company from destroying a native burial ground.

Even the lounge suite had a history, for it had once resided in a royal palace. As Florrie sat on the couch and listened to Ada's recitation, she had no idea that her backside was gracing the same furniture as other regal posteriors.

Ada herself was ensconced in her armchair, her hands wrapped around a mug of tea. The journey home had been harrowing. Like an old Marconi wireless set, every time the train had crossed tracks or points, her hip had telegraphed a message of pain. As a consequence, when she'd alighted at King's Cross Station, the walking stick had finally been put to proper use.

Upon arriving home, she had made a pot of tea, taken two tablets, dropped with relief into the armchair, telephoned Florrie to say that she was home, and rested her leg on a footstool.

The black lacquered legs were of oriental design and at least two hundred years old. However, the upholstered cushion was a replacement. As Ada well knew, the original cover was tucked away in a government vault, for whoever had embroidered the intricate pattern had incorporated a deadly secret.

"So, it was the money they were after?" said Florrie. "What a pair of...um...I don't like using bad language. Give me one of your perky words."

Ada chuckled. "I can think of quite a few but none would be adequate. The Inspector said he would contact me in the next few days, and no doubt I'll learn more then. But, yes, money was the motive."

During the journey home, Ada had given considerable thought as to what she would tell Florrie. She might be cantankerous at times but she was no fool. It was one thing to question a stranger, but quite another when it was one's lifelong friend.

In addition, ever since Frank's death, Ada always felt somewhat adrift when she returned from a 'job'. Not being able to discuss her work was something she missed, for it helped her relax and put things in perspective. She could not tell Florrie everything, and if she became too inquisitive, then all she, Ada, had to do, was fudge it.

"Let me get this right," said Florrie, valiantly putting the pieces together. "Mirabelle Ayres or Davenport as she was known, conveniently died before she could make a claim against her late father's estate. Katherine Wilson was killed with sleeping pills by mistake, the brothers thinking her Elizabeth, who in turn, when she realised they'd killed the wrong woman, tried to pass herself off as her sister."

"Not quite. Katherine's death is still being investigated, and there were a lot of empty capsules by her bed. But in my opinion, one or both of the brothers mixed the contents in a drink and forced it down her throat." Ada smiled as she mischievously added, "After that, Elizabeth became quite disquiparant."

Florrie rolled her eyes. "I'm not even going to ask what that means. Do you want a refill?"

Ada held out the now empty cup. Florrie went into the kitchen and switched the kettle on. In reality, the tea making was an excuse to give her time to think.

She had known from the outset that something was different, primarily because Ada had not stopped talking since she, Florrie, walked through the door. Was it simply a case of 'getting it off her chest', or was Ada finally about to 'come clean'?

She was far too savvy to be bullied into a confession, and direct questions would put her on her guard. Florrie decided to wait and listen, and where she could without arousing suspicion, encourage rather than confront.

"From what you said earlier," she said while handing Ada a fresh mug of tea, "if the brothers mistook one sister for the other, they must have looked very alike."

"There was a slight resemblance, but according to Mrs Osborne from the haberdasher's, Mirabelle and Elizabeth looked more like sisters than she and Katherine. Having had a long career in the theatre, Elizabeth knew exactly how to alter her appearance."

"How did you catch her out?"

"Well, for all her experience, there was one feature that Elizabeth could not disguise, and in a roundabout way, the first clue came from you."

"Me? How?"

"Do you remember when you got your new glasses?"

"I'd rather not."

"When Elizabeth went bonkers over her sister's jewellery, her bulging eyes reminded me of what you'd said in the optometrist's - 'I look like a frog'. I didn't think anything of it at the time, and then I remembered the word I'd used - batrachian - frog like - green! Katherine had blue eyes but Elizabeth's were green.

"No doubt if she'd thought of it, she'd have used coloured contact lenses, but as she was too busy trying to stay alive, the mistake was easily made."

"And then there was the stage make-up. When I first went to Elizabeth's room after Katherine died, the only place to sit down was on a footstool. It had a bit of powder on the top, and thinking it talcum, I brushed it away and wiped my hand on my dress.

"Later, I realised it was theatrical make-up. I suppose in her haste to effect a disguise, Elizabeth did not notice that some of the powder had fallen on the footstool."

"How can you tell the difference?"

"Theatrical powder is much thicker and heavier than normal face powder. It is also quite greasy, hence the term 'grease paint'.

"There was one more difference. Elizabeth spoke with what you would call 'a plum in the mouth posh accent' and rarely used contracted words. For example, she would say 'do not' as opposed to 'don't'."

Florrie nodded in understanding. "It would be like me trying to speak in a French accent. As soon as I opened my mouth you'd know I was a cockney. When something is part of who you are, it's very difficult to change it."

Ada was impressed. "You sound like a psychiatrist."

"Huh, I might not be the brightest light in the street but I'm not the dimmest either." Satisfied that she'd made her point, Florrie returned to the former subject. "Did Elizabeth wear her sister's clothes as well?"

"Hmm, not that I noticed. Not that it mattered. The brooch was the ultimate betrayer."

"Brooch? What brooch?"

"Oh, didn't I mention it? It was shaped like an Egyptian cartouche and had a scarab in the centre. Katherine told me while we were having drinks on Sunday evening that she wore it all the time, and yet after her death, whenever I saw Elizabeth, she always held a handkerchief to her face.

"She later admitted that in her panic, she'd forgotten to remove the brooch from her sister's clothes. On one occasion, she opened the door in a stooping position to disguise the discrepancy in their height."

"I bet when she retired from the theatre, she never thought she'd use her experience again, at least, not in such a manner."

Florrie paused to drink her tea, and then asked a question that, while perfectly natural under the circumstances, could also be construed as 'leading'. "By the way, all those enquiries I made for you, where do they fit in?"

Ada did not answer immediately. Instead, she shifted her position and resettled her leg on the footstool. Like Florrie, she was also stalling for time. They were sailing into uncharted waters, and yet the temptation to answer truthfully was hard to resist.

So far, she had explained her involvement as mere chance. The question now was, how much did she want to hide? The answer if she was honest was, 'not much'.

Perhaps she would talk to Bert about it when she saw him next week. In the meantime, she could only speak judiciously. She therefore borrowed her answer from Mr Travis.

"You see it all the time on the telly. Whenever there's an investigation, the first thing the cops do is establish who is who. I hadn't been in the hotel thirty seconds when I heard Elizabeth complaining about the Major to Cedric Ayres - at least, I think it was him.

"Later that evening when I became acquainted with the sisters, Elizabeth warned me against the Major. Yet that same evening when I had dinner with him, I found him charming and amusing, which completely contradicted her opinion.

"Call me nosey but my curiosity was roused, hence why I asked you to look-up those records." She added sincerely, "I'm sorry I lied to you."

Florrie flapped a hand dismissively. "Never mind about that. Did the information help?"

"It was of tremendous importance, but in order to understand the relevance, it's probably best to look at the situation from the Major's point of view.

"He is a bachelor enjoying his retirement, then out of the blue, he's contacted by a long lost cousin. Even more astonishing, she's residing at the same hotel he's been visiting for years.

"He goes to meet her, only to discover that she's died under appalling circumstances. He wants to get to the bottom of it, but he doesn't want anyone to know the real reason for his visit. Now, under those circumstances, what would you do?"

Florrie thought for a moment and then admitted, "I have no idea."

"The short answer is – nothing. As he's been visiting the hotel for years, his presence there is not unusual. He bides his time, hoping something will surface. And then a nosey parker by the name of Ada Harris starts asking questions. He has no idea who she is, and not wanting to disclose his relationship to Mirabelle, he keeps his mouth shut."

Florrie clicked her fingers. "I can see a flaw in that. What if he lured her to the hotel himself? His entire story could be a pack of lies. He hears about the redevelopment project, puts two & two together, and arranges to meet her at the hotel."

Ada grinned. "I love your cynicism, Florrie, but you're overlooking an important point. Mirabelle emigrated with her mother and was never heard of again."

"Huh, so he says. They could have been in contact for years. In fact, the whole idea could have been his. Of course, he couldn't have known what was going to happen afterwards, but that doesn't mean he didn't lure her there."

Ada laughed. "You're making him sound like a master criminal. He was telling the truth because the events and other facts confirmed his story. Besides, his reaction when I showed him the note was genuine."

Florrie let out a sigh of exasperation. "What note? How am I supposed to keep the story straight if you keep missing bits out?"

Ada retrieved her handbag and extracted the note. Florrie read it and then said sarcastically, "Charming. It must have taken a sick mind to write it."

"Yes," replied Ada, suddenly speaking distractedly. "Mr Travis made a similar comment when he read it." She would never be able to call him by his proper name. To her, he would always be Mr Travis.

Florrie, the offensive missive still in her hand, looked up sharply. "What's the matter? Why do you sound uncertain?"

"Because there are pieces of the puzzle that don't fit."

"Such as?"

"Such as Elizabeth and her pendulous personality. That means…"

"I know what it means! I'm not a complete imbecile."

Ada sat back and rested her hands on her tummy. "Alright, Sherlock, figure this one out. There was definitely underlying tension between the sisters, and on at least three occasions, Elizabeth severely checked her sister. I don't mean a polite 'Sorry, dear, but you're wrong'. No, she really snapped at her.

"In addition, she became really apprehensive every time her sister opened her mouth. It was as if she was afraid Katherine was about to say something she shouldn't."

Florrie twisted her mouth as she thought of an answer. "Perhaps when Elizabeth snapped at her sister, she was in a bad mood."

Ada grunted. "If that was the case, then I would say Elizabeth has been in a bad mood for years."

"Perhaps she suffers from some sort of personality disorder."

"I thought of that too, and yet after Katherine's death, Elizabeth seemed to settle down. And here's another conundrum. Why, after her meeting with Alistair Walsh, did Miss Davenport give the jewellery box to Elizabeth? Mirabelle must have known what was hidden inside, so why relinquish it?"

"As a means of keeping it from the brothers."

"Yes, but why bring it into the hotel at all? Why not leave it with Alistair Walsh?"

"You said earlier that Mr Travis and others described Miss Davenport as a sweet little old lady. She wants to keep things amicable between herself and her brothers, but they don't believe who she is, and when she says she can prove it, they persuade her to bring her birth certificate to the hotel.

"She retrieves the box from Alistair Walsh and then has a discussion with her brothers. But, it doesn't go well. She is very frightened, and during dinner, asks Elizabeth to accompany her to her room."

Ada did not respond immediately. It had occurred to her that she was discussing the case more fully than intended. Although the flow of conversation was perfectly natural, she felt she must close it down until she spoke to Bert.

"That was my interpretation too, and it certainly fits the known facts. But, with so much at stake, it would have been safer to show the brothers a photocopy. I am absolutely sure there's a piece of the story that's missing, but I'm darned if I know what it is."

Florrie looked at her pityingly. "Perhaps you could ask the Inspector."

"Maybe." Ada shrugged. "What's on telly tonight?"

Chapter 23. A Few Days Later.

If there was one foible that Florrie had maintained throughout her life, it was her propensity for slamming doors. The unprovoked attack on paint and woodwork was always accompanied by a superfluous shout of, "It's me!"

Much to her chagrin, Ada had never been able to break her friend of the habit, and when Florrie 'announced' her arrival with more than her usual gusto, the resulting 'bang' could have been heard two streets away.

She bounded into the lounge room, her handbag swinging on her arm. "You'll never guess what I found out."

"You're right - I couldn't guess."

"Do you know where the keyboard comes from?"

"Taiwan? South Korea?"

"No - the design. It comes from the typewriter, which was first patented in 1868 by Christopher Latham Scholes."

Ada raised an eyebrow. "That early? I thought it was much later than that."

"So do most people," responded Florrie, throwing both herself and her handbag on the former royal couch. "The first machines only had capital letters, and the rows were set out in alphabetical order. Well, he didn't sell too many of 'em till he changed the layout, which is still the current format."

"What's that in your hand?" asked Ada.

"Oh - I forgot. There was a courier on the doorstep when I arrived. She held out a small parcel. "I signed for it."

Ada's name and address were written on a half sheet of notepaper taped to the front, the printed address at the top being The Seabridge Hotel.

Ada removed the outer wrapping, exposing a bulky envelope and a brown velvet box. "Florrie! This is it! This is the jewellery box where Miss Davenport hid her birth certificate."

Florrie was equally agog. "Is there anything in it?"

Ada raised the lid. Her eyes widened when she saw Katherine's brooch. The red scarab in the centre seemed to look back at her as though to say, 'what else were you expecting?'

"I don't understand this," she said, giving it to Florrie, who knowing its fatal background, handled it with reverential care.

"You were right about it being strange. It's rather macabre in its way." Florrie turned it over. "There's some initials on the back."

Ada extracted two smaller envelopes from the bulky one. "Probably something 'W'. I don't think they ever said what their mother's Christian name was."

"No, its not. The initials are 'M.D'."

Her focus being on the envelopes, it took Ada a moment to comprehend what Florrie had said. "What? It can't be."

"The engraving is old and worn but still legible." Seeing the utter incomprehension on Ada's

235

face, Florrie pointed to one of the envelopes. "Open that one first. It has an emblem and looks official."

Somewhat dazedly, Ada slit the flap. It did not occur to her until later that, rather than a computer, Inspector Butler had written the letter by hand. Somehow, it seemed to convey that, not only did he regret being unable to deliver his news in person, but that he did not want to leave an electronic trail.

Dear Mrs Harris,

Before I begin, I must state at the outset that the opinions expressed in this letter are my own and not those of the Upper Markham constabulary.

It is with deep regret that I inform you of the death of Elizabeth Wilson. It would appear that, following your recitation on Thursday last, she returned to her room and committed suicide.

When she did not emerge for dinner, the Major became concerned and sent Travis to her room. He knocked, and when there was no reply, he opened the door, which was unlocked.

At the risk of sounding dramatic, she died like a queen, in that she was laid on the bed with her arms crossed over her chest. The Major's childhood photograph was in her hand. I remember him giving it to her when we were all in the cocktail lounge, but I think he forgot to take it back.

Do not be alarmed. It is not a case of history repeating itself. On the contrary, she left a letter, a photocopy of which is enclosed. As per her instructions, I am sending you the jewellery box and the brooch. I will execute the remainder of her instructions personally.

There have been several developments since you left, which I have no doubt you will be interested to know. It took two days of interrogation but eventually the Ayres brothers cracked. I've met some tough villains in my time, but the belligerence and arrogance of the brothers was extraordinary.

They claimed that they were protecting their father's legacy, which given that the hotel was about to be sold for an obscene amount of money, is complete nonsense. Further, they asserted that Miss Davenport's death was an accident, and that Miss Katherine's was self-defence.

Their solicitor is one of those pompous London 'suits' who think they know the law backwards. I am not the least concerned. The evidence, coupled with Miss Elizabeth's suicide letter, will secure murder convictions. I have also charged Cedric Ayres with the attempted murder of your good self.

It was good thinking to place Travis in the room across the corridor where he could keep an eye on your door. As the Major said, 'you took a hell of a risk', though I suspect it wasn't your first.

I have also charged the brothers with six counts of 'public nuisance' in relation to the practical jokes. The Major and Travis are being very co-operative in this regard, and while it is highly likely that more charges will be laid, there is no evidence to connect the brothers to the murder of Alistair Walsh.

The Major has already consulted a solicitor and has lodged an injunction against the brothers. In the interim, he and Travis will run the hotel as a going concern. They already have an eye to refurbishment in regard to next year's summer season.

As an entity, Breakaway Constructions have been cleared of any involvement. However, there is a side issue that I thought rather amusing. As part of the negotiating process, and no doubt to curry favour, the brothers had allowed Mr Tomlinson and his secretary to stay at the hotel, gratis. Not anymore. The Major told the developer to either start paying or get out.

As you correctly deduced, the sale of the hotel was subject to vacant possession, and Mr Tomlinson was not pleased to learn that it is now subject to an inheritance claim, which until the matter is settle, suspends his agreement with the brothers.

You have to give him credit for audacity. He approached the Major with a view to selling his share, and was - pardon the pun, sent packing.

By rights, I should charge Mrs Osborne with withholding evidence, but as I said to Travis, 'It's not worth the paperwork'. Nevertheless, I did give her a 'friendly' warning about complying with the law. Would you believe she had the audacity to try and sell me a lamp with a hideous brown base.

The amusement arcade will close at the end of next week, and once it is bulldozed, a department store will be built on the site. Though it will provide much needed employment in the area, I cannot help but wonder if, for the new owner's, it's a case of exchanging one fountain of money for another. What price progress, eh? And yes, this time the pun was intended.

We had another storm on Saturday night. It was nothing like the one we had last Thursday, but it was too much for the old pier. It broke apart and collapsed into the sea, and on the following afternoon, a dog walker reported seeing an unexploded bomb in the wreckage. Turned out to be an old sewage pipe, which rather sums up the situation.

You will need to return and give evidence in regard to the attempted murder charge, but I don't think you will have any problem obtaining accommodation. Which reminds me, the Major asked me to tell you that lamb shanks are now on the menu. I presume you know what he means.

Yours sincerely,
Raymond Butler.

Ada put the letter in her lap and buried her face in her hands. Her voice trembled as she said, "Florrie, there's a bottle of whiskey in the sideboard. Pour me a drink."

Florrie tactfully refrained from mentioning that it wasn't 11 o'clock yet. Not since the death of Frank Harris had she seen Ada so upset. Feeling rather helpless, Florrie poured the requested restorative and exchanged it for the Inspector's letter.

She read it carefully and then looked at her friend. "Oh, Ada, what a terrible turn of events."

Engulfed by sadness and an overwhelming sense of failure, Ada held out the second letter.

"Read it aloud." Florrie opened the envelope and cleared her throat.

***

The silence was palpable as Florrie's voice, which had steadily grown sombre, came to a halt. There was a peculiar wheezing noise, and then Ada roared with laughter, her ample frame shifting and rocking with the force of tectonic plates.

Florrie could not have looked more surprised if she'd won the lottery without buying a ticket. "Ada! This is a terrible letter. Why are you laughing?"

Ada could hardly get the words out. "Because it's a letter from arguably the greatest actress in the world."

"You mean it's a fake!" Florrie's eyes were almost popping out of her head, the air crackling with outrage. "After everything you went through, after you almost got yourself killed, are you saying that the first victim wasn't a victim at all?"

Ada wiped her streaming eyes. "I don't know," she spluttered between guffaws, her voice sounding like a gangster's machine gun. "On the other hand, we'll never know."

Florrie could not see what was so funny. She did, however, see an opening that was too good to miss. She took a deep breath and adopted her best 'don't mess with me' tone.

"Speaking of actresses and believing things, I'm no ballistics expert, Ada, but why does your Russian samovar have a bullet hole in the base?"

Chapter 24. A Letter From the Dead.

Dear Inspector Butler,

Unlike your good self, I am not conversant with the law in regard to deathbed confessions. Therefore, to avoid any potential complication or misunderstanding, I would like it firmly understood that I make this statement of my own free will.

My correct name is Mirabelle Ayres, and I am the instrument by which three innocent people lost their lives. I do not propose to make excuses, but provide explanations that will give you an understanding of my actions.

Further, although Ada was essentially correct in her narrative earlier today, there are several points I feel compelled to elaborate, correct, or clarify, as the case may be.

I will not dwell on my time in Australia nor the years thereafter. They have no relevance to my story. Nor does the reason why, upon returning to England in 1969, I used my mother's maiden name of Davenport.

Suffice to say that I had never forgotten my former home, and upon arriving at the hotel, Travis took my registration. He escorted me to the lift, and just as the doors were closing, I saw Cedric emerge from the office. To discover he was still alive and the hotel still in the family, came as a complete surprise.

To calm my tumultuous mind, I read the local newspaper that Travis had given me upon arrival. It contained a substantial article on the town's redevelopment, and how Breakaway Constructions were already looking to expand the project.

I remember looking at my watch. It was just after ten am. As Ada generously complimented, I am not a particularly stupid or senile person, and given the passage of time, it was safe to assume that my father, William Frederick Ayres, was dead.

After much consideration and reflection, I telephoned a friend who gave me the details of a solicitor - Alistair Walsh. I telephoned and requested an urgent appointment, and by two o'clock that afternoon was in his office.

My circumstances having been explained, Mr Walsh advised that a search should be undertaken to discover if my father had left a Will. As the matter had potential for substantial financial gain, he also advised that I should vacate the hotel immediately, thereby preventing my identity being known before we were ready to proceed.

I informed him that, after decades of working in the theatre, I was more than capable of disguising myself. For the benefit of Ada, everything I stated about my life in the theatre on Sunday evening was true. I really was speaking from experience, which I did on another occasion, which I will come to presently.

I obtained the necessary theatrical supplies and went to a hotel for tea. Afterwards, when I was utilising their facilities to create my disguise, a thought occurred to me. While it is true that my stepbrothers played tricks on guests, I was also the victim of their puerile pranks. Therefore, a disguise would afford me an opportunity to determine what type of men they had become.

When I returned that evening, I looked like a different woman. Remember, Travis was the only person who had seen my initial arrival at the hotel, and there had not been enough time for him to commit my features to memory.

The following day, I saw that the disguise I had created was almost identical to the natural appearance of Elizabeth Wilson, and over the ensuing weeks, I was often mistaken for her sister instead of Katherine.

We became good friends, and when a nasty trick was played on the real Elizabeth, I recognized my stepbrothers' handiwork. I should state at this point that I did not make the connection between the jokes and the sale of the hotel.

How did I know my stepbrothers were the culprits? As young boys, they played tricks on the guests, and I sometimes contributed to the antics. But then I realised the pranks were hurtful and tried to persuade Cedric and Herbert to stop.

But, to continue. I had kept in regular contact with Mr Walsh by telephone, and eventually, he informed me about the clause in my father's Will. He also informed me that, while there was a record of my parent's marriage, there was none of my birth. Apparently, a number of books, registers, and other documents did not survive the war.

I asked that the matter be left in abeyance. I am not a vindictive woman, and before anything of a legal nature occurred, I wanted to expose my stepbrothers' cruelty. But, how to do it without revealing my identity? The answer was literally staring me in the face.

I summoned the sisters to my room, and under the pretext of a plan to catch the joker, persuaded Elizabeth to adopt a disguise, to wit, my own natural appearance. As far as she was concerned, our supposed similarity was a quirk of nature.

Elizabeth approached Cedric at the reception desk and declared herself to be Mirabelle Davenport. Naturally he did not believe her. However, when she recited anecdotes and stated that there was documentary proof, (all fake as far as she was concerned), his manner instantly changed.

He invited her into his office for a chat, and when she enquired as to the whereabouts of Herbert, he said he did not know. When Elizabeth repeated the conversation to me, I knew with absolute certainty that Cedric had lied.

Although Ada named two differences in character, I knew a third. For the short time we all lived under the one roof, Herbert fell off his bike and hurt his neck, leaving a small scar under his right ear. Hence how I knew he was in the hotel.

In the days following Cedric's ridiculous denial, I upped the ante and paraded the false Miss Davenport at every opportunity. Moreover, her penchant for knitting in the cocktail lounge was pure theatre.

A point of clarification. My statement that 'Miss Davenport' returned with the box after meeting Mr Walsh, and her request that she be escorted to her room after dinner, are a complete fabrication. The box and document were in my possession the entire time. Mr Walsh had made a photocopy the only time I was in his office.

Driven by greed and desperation, the latter no doubt promulgated by 'Miss Davenport's'' constant presence in the hotel, my stepbrothers committed murder.

If you will pardon a modicum of egotism, I have always enjoyed a strong constitution. It was certainly needed on the morning I found her dead, for in spite of my statement to the contrary, I did in fact enter her room. The manner of her death was vile and degrading, and it was from this that I deduced the 'why' and the 'who'.

After the real Elizabeth died, for my own safety, I had no choice but to maintain her persona. But, Katherine began to believe that I really was her sister, and that it was 'Miss Davenport' who had died.

Did I feel guilt or remorse? Of course I did, but revealing the secret would not achieve anything. Better and arguably kinder for Katherine that I maintain the deception.

Yet I could not trust her, for she frequently lapsed into bouts of severe melancholy. I used my sleeping pills to keep her quiet, covertly administering them whenever she became distressed.

Unfortunately, the method was not foolproof, and every now and then the sedation failed. Ada was witness to one of these bouts when Katherine spoke about her brooch in the cocktail lounge.

If it is any consolation to you, Ada, our walk on Monday morning afforded me the opportunity to recall those halcyon days when life was much simpler. I thank you for that. I also agree with your reconstruction of Katherine's death. However, you were not entirely correct.

After Katherine and I exchanged rooms, she had a headache and lay down on her 'new' bed. Later, I realised I had not removed my possessions from my former bedside drawer, which included the jewellery box and sleeping pills.

When she did not emerge for tea, I knocked on her door several times. There was no response, and so I tried the handle. It was unlocked. The curtains were drawn and I turned on the light.

At first, I thought she was asleep. And then I saw the empty capsules by the bed. I thought she had taken an overdose, but one touch was enough to confirm she was still alive.

I looked at the pathetic creature and felt utterly ashamed. If it had not been for my vanity and curiosity, Elizabeth would still be alive. I knew then it would be impossible to keep Katherine constantly sedated, and so I took the pillow and ended her life.

As I returned to my room, it struck me that perhaps it had not been an overdose. I suddenly felt very cold. Was history repeating itself? The real Elizabeth had died in my stead. Had Katherine suffered the fate that should have been mine?

As Ada stated on a number of occasions, she was the only person who knew we were exchanging rooms. It had to be more than coincidence, as was the death of Alistair Walsh. Yes, I had already made that connection. My stepbrothers had killed twice, so why not a third time?

I was awake all night in fear. There was every chance my stepbrothers would realise their mistake and come for me during the night. I would most certainly be powerless against them. I considered relinquishing my claim by giving them my birth certificate, but considering they had already murdered twice, my prospects of leaving the hotel alive were virtually non-existent.

There was an inescapable irony, in that the brothers would need to be summoned to Katherine's room. If, however, upon seeing me still in the guise of Elizabeth, they realised their mistake - assuming they had not done so beforehand, there was no telling what they might do. I therefore changed my identity again.

I drew comfort from the fact that, while the police were in the hotel, my stepbrothers would not attempt anything. Even so, the box was still in Katherine's room and I had no opportunity to retrieve it.

By the time Ada came to see me on Tuesday evening, I was almost senseless with anxiety. My birth certificate was proving a death sentence for whoever possessed it, and yet its retrieval was vital. Ada unwittingly provided the method when she asked if there was anything she could do.

I had intended to vacate the hotel forthwith, the story about Wales being another lie. However, when Ada intervened and took charge of the box, I was more than happy to acquiesce, naively believing that my secret would not be discovered and that the box would be returned in time. With the benefit of hindsight, I should have told the truth from the start, but self-preservation was dominating rational thought.

When the certificate was produced during Ada's recitation, I was shocked to say the least. To have the bare bones of my life exposed in the third person was a surreal experience. Further, when Travis gave me the note to read, I thought I was undone. I do not require glasses, whereas the real Elizabeth did. The prescription is quite strong, hence why I pretended not to have the glasses with me.

I must now address another painful subject, to wit, my persecution of Major Eaton. I had completely forgotten about my cousin, and it was while Mr Walsh was conducting his enquiries that the Major's name came up. Being ex-army, he was relatively easy to find, and when I managed to contact him at his club, like him, I was astounded to discover our relationship to the hotel.

He agreed to meet me but arrived too late. The fake 'Miss Davenport' was dead, and having assumed Elizabeth's identity, I could not reveal who I really was.

I deeply regret not acknowledging or renewing our relationship. Nor did the prospect of him inheriting my portion of the hotel occur to me. I now remedy this oversight by bequeathing him my portion entirely. If he chooses, he may regard it as recompense for my disgraceful behaviour. I apologise unreservedly, and hope he will find it in his kind heart to forgive me.

Please ensure Ada receives the jewellery box and Katherine's brooch, the other jewellery to be donated to a theatrical company of your choice. The remainder of my possessions and money are to be given to charity.

Nothing can compensate for the unnecessary and untimely deaths of two loving sisters and a fine solicitor. I have taken steps to atone for it. It is absolute and irreversible and I willingly pay the price. There are other points I should cover, but if you would forgive me, Inspector, I am feeling rather drowsy.

I bid you farewell, and in particular, the excellent Mrs Harris. Please convey my heartfelt gratitude for taking such good care of me during my last days.

Yours in memoriam,
Mirabelle Davenport.

Epilogue.

The lane was so narrow that the mirrors of the taxi almost scraped the walls. "Are you sure this is the right place?" asked the driver nervously, the closeness almost giving him claustrophobia.

"Oh, yes," replied Ada, completely unperturbed. "Turn right at the end and then stop."

"It'll be a swine to reverse."

"You don't need to. The lane runs in an arc and brings you back to the main road."

"Good," he commented, sounding very relieved.

He followed Ada's directions, and after paying the fare, she entered a building that seemed buried amidst a concrete jungle. Surrounded by high-rise offices and apartments, the front steps of the grey, non-descript building were well worn, and pending on the time of year and the angle of the sun, a brass plaque by the door with the name 'Clean 4U' occasionally shone.

"Hello, Sir Figgins," she said cheerfully to the aged concierge, but this was not his real name.

Some sixty years earlier, his heavily pregnant mother had been 'taking tea' in a café called Figgins when, to everyone's surprise, especially her own, her water broke. A minor royal had been sitting at a nearby table, and in the spirit of 'noblesse oblige', he had helped her give birth. The resulting son had henceforth been known as Sir Figgins, with his real name known only to a few.

"Nice to see you again, Mrs H. You are expected so just go straight up."

Ada crossed a small foyer to the lift. It looked even more antiquated than the one installed at the Seabridge Hotel, but this was only for the sake of appearance. Not only was the building reinforced to withstand a rocket attack, but was wired with the most advanced surveillance equipment that would never be commercially available.

Ada alighted on the third floor and walked along a corridor, not caring that a dozen pair of electronic eyes were watching her every move. She knocked on a plain wooden door and was bidden to enter.

Bert rose from behind his desk and held out a hand. "Ah, Ada, good to see you. Take a seat."

Ada sat down and automatically unbuttoned her coat. Albert Eagles hated the cold and his office was always like a hothouse. It resembled one as well. The orchids by the window would have taken first prize at any flower show, while the 'Bizzie Lizzie' on top of a bookcase looked positively dangerous.

"I have read your report," he said. "Detailed and thorough as usual."

"No, its not, there's a post-script. Caroline McGuiness is safe and well. Apparently, she'd had enough of pandering to little old ladies in the haberdashers, and is now training to be an assistant in one of the new supermarkets."

Bert unscrewed the top of his fountain pen - he rarely wrote with anything else, and made a note on the report. He then sat back and folded his hands. "What I am more interested in is why it's so clinical."

Ada frowned. "I don't know what you mean."

"Ordinarily, your reports are like a thriller novel - suspenseful, adventurous, and not without humour. This..." he picked up the report and then tossed it back on the desk, "is like reading a prescription for laxatives. I know you far too well. I can tell you have a problem. So, come on, out with it."

Ada sighed heavily. She had always admired Bert's power of perception, which sometimes bordered on the supernatural. Ergo, there was no point trying to deceive him. "Two problems," she confessed.

"And the first?"

"My aged, addled brain cost Katherine Wilson her life. I was too slow. I didn't put the pieces together fast enough."

Bert sat back in his chair, and instead of being serious and grim, he smiled in bemusement. "Oh, that old chestnut. I've had operators as young as thirty come to me with a similar problem, so I will tell you the same thing I told them. You can only work with what is to hand. If a situation is unclear and something unfortunate or unforeseen happens, you can't blame yourself."

"But that's the point. The facts were to hand. I just didn't put them together in time."

"So?" he said laconically, as if the subject was of minor importance, even a little irritating.

Ada stared at her boss. Was he being callous? No, of course he wasn't. In his own inimitable style, he was making her confront her doubt.

"So, what am I supposed to do about it?" she asked.

"What do you want to do?" he shot back.

Ada growled in frustration. "I hate it when you go Freudian on me."

"Ada," he said patiently, "you are asking me to supply an answer you already possess." He tapped his temple. "The solution is already in your head. All you have to do is think about it. Now, what is the second problem?"

"Florrie. I think she knows."

Albert Eagles, the 'Mr-Fix It man of the government', burst out laughing. "Oh, Ada," he said, holding up his hands as though ready to fend off an attack, "if you're seriously trying to tell me that you've only just realised that Mrs Brown has cottoned on to you, then I'm afraid you've been losing your touch for years."

"But, aren't you concerned that her knowledge might compromise security?"

"Of course not. If I remember rightly, Mrs Brown was first vetted many years ago. We do not usually involve ourselves in domestic disputes, but my father thought so highly of you and Frank, that when you contacted him in relation to Ted Brown, he called in a favour. Did you never wonder why Ted Brown was arrested so quickly?"

Ada cast her mind back to the night when, battered and freezing to death, Florrie and her children had appeared on the doorstep. "I was a very naïve operative back then," she admitted. "I think the American phrase is 'green horn'.

"Florrie was in such a terrible state that I had to do something. I telephoned your father and he said

253

he would take care of it. I had no idea he went to such lengths."

Bert smiled in understanding. "Since then, Mrs Brown has regularly undergone what I might euphemistically term, a social check-up."

Ada did not know whether to be grateful or annoyed. "You mean you've probed into her private life?"

"Yes. Oh, nothing overly intrusive - just the usual political and activist organisations."

Ada started to laugh. "Florrie? An activist? The only activism she's interested in is grumbling, complaining, and voicing her opinion."

"None of which are subversive, at least not yet. Mrs Brown is not a threat to national security."

"Except when she's trying to use a library card as a bus pass."

Ada explained about Florrie's old glasses. Bert grinned and then said, "Mrs Brown is a rare commodity these days - a true friend. The bond of trust you shared with Frank was absolute, and human nature being what it is, his death has left an emotional hole in your heart.

"In regard to your work, Mrs Brown can go part of the way to filling that hole. I'm not suggesting you divulge everything to her - we both know that's not possible, but should you choose to do so, you can involve her in a peripheral sense. Believe me, if I was in any way concerned about Mrs Brown, I would have retired you years ago."

Ada felt her stomach tighten. There it was, the dreaded 'R' word. She looked at him warily. Had he said it deliberately? Was he offering her a way out despite his advice? Perhaps it wouldn't hurt to probe the subject.

"Speaking of retirement," she said tentatively, "that same thought has crossed my mind of late. I'm getting a bit long in the tooth and I don't think Frank would have wanted me to continue."

Bert slowly shook his head. "The only reason you're thinking of retiring is because you believe you failed in Upper Markham. How long is it since you've seen your family?"

The question took Ada by surprise, but there again, Bert was very good at catching people unawares. "I speak to them regularly but I haven't actually seen them for about 18 months." She looked at him suspiciously. "Why do you ask?"

"Because I think you need, to use another Americanism, 'time out'. Ordinarily, my remedy for a lack of confidence would be to throw the operative back into the deep end. This method might sound cruel but it works in eight out of ten cases. Self-recrimination, reflective post-mortems, negative speculation, anything that contributes to the lessening of efficiency are luxuries this department cannot afford.

"In your case, you're not suffering from a lack of confidence, you're suffering from a sense of failure, and they are very different things. A woman died and you feel an overwhelming sense of responsibility. Well, to use a vulgarity, bullshit.

"Based on the facts you had to hand, you might have anticipated what the brothers' would do, but you could never have guessed what Miss Ayres, AKA Miss Davenport, would do. You could no

255

more have prevented Katherine's death than you could stop the sun from shining.

"In my opinion, you need time to reconcile the events. So, take my advice - get on a plane and go visit your family. A change of scenery will do you the world of good."

Ada burst out laughing. "It was the doctor saying the same thing to me last week that started all this."

Bert did not reply. Instead, he scribbled a note, sealed it in an envelope, and held it out. "Take this to the travel section. Call it Doctor Eagles's cure for a bout of despondency."

"Thanks, Bert." Ada put the envelope in a coat pocket and stood up to leave. His pep talk, whilst not exactly alleviating her doubts, had made her feel a little better.

She was about to speak and then saw it was pointless. Bert's eyes were fixed on a sheet of paper. He had already turned his attention to something else. She walked to the door and was about to open it when he spoke from behind.

"By the way, I had you earmarked for a cushy job next week, but as you won't be here to do it, I'll have to assign it to someone else."

"A cushy job?" she repeated sceptically. "The last time you described a job as 'cushy', I ended up being chased across the Alaskan tundra on a skidoo. It took weeks for my bones to thaw out."

"Ah, yes, that was most unfortunate, but this one really is cushy. It's a simple baby-sitting job and involves two girls at an exclusive boarding school in the country. One girl is the daughter of a notorious mobster, and the other is the daughter of the man who's about to give evidence against him.

"Pity you'll be away. You could have asked Mrs Brown to help babysit the girls." Bert picked up a yellow folder, one of the many on his desk. "Oh, well, never mind. Enjoy your holiday."

***

Ada walked along the corridor to the lift, her steps slow and her mind thoughtful. Why had Bert mentioned a job she would not be doing? Nor was he a man who gave up easily. And what was in the envelope?

She slit it open and read the note. "Why, that cunning old..." She turned around, looked at his door, and burst into hearty laughter.

The note read: 'Take a trip to the country, followed by a first-class flight to Australia - both at departmental expense.

THE END.

Other Books & Freebies.

NON-FICTION.

The Politically Incorrect Dictionary: a fun look at alternative meanings of words. Packed with trivia and information.

The Naughty Dictionary: this is a companion piece to the above, and consists entirely of vulgarisms dating back centuries. WARNING! Parental guidance is recommended for children under 16.

FICTION.

£5 MURDER: crime.
A DOSE OF FAMILIARITY: romance.
A GOOD DEED: ghost.
ANALYSIS OF A HAT: classic Sherlock Holmes.
BAIT: Some people will do just about anything for money. Humour. (Also known as 'FOR SALE'.)
BLACKMAIL BY PROXY: crime.
CHAMELEON – THE DEATH OF SHERLOCK HOLMES: Classic Crime.
GOD OF DRUNKS: humour/romance.
KANGARA: (general fiction): Mysticism clashes with the wisdom of an old colonel.
FOOL'S GOLD: humour.
LABOURED JUSTICE: crime.

MISTRESS OF DEATH: Female Crime.

ORCHARD OF DREAMS: romance/ghost.

PEARLS BEFORE SWINE: crime.

PRINCE FOR A NIGHT: crime.

THE BEST CUT: classic Sherlock Holmes.

THE BLACK PHANTOM: A family legend proves very real.

THE CURSED BROOCH: classic Sherlock Holmes.

THE FAILURES OF SHERLOCK HOLMES: Whilst desperately ill and in a fevered state, Holmes is haunted by some of his less celebrated cases, including a second encounter with 'THE' woman, Irene Adler.

THE FAVOUR: Ghost/Romance.

THE FIXER: General fiction - a stranger's tragic tale has unexpected consequences.

THE PACKING CASE MURDER: classic Sherlock Holmes.

THE RIGHT ORDER: romance.

THE SACRIFICE: Historical romance. 643 AD, and Egypt is at a political crossroads. The Romans have come and gone, the Greeks have been usurped by the Muslims, and Christianity is on the march. But there are still those who believe in the power of the Pharaohs, and when a displaced girl searches for her missing father, the resulting clash of cultures leads to murder, madness, and mobocracy.

THE SISTERHOOD – CURSE OF ABBOT HEWITT: Who said all the members of a covenant were the best of friends? Adult horror/historical. (Note: Due to breach of contract for the non-

THE SISTERHOOD – CATHY'S KIN: sequel to Curse of Abbot Hewitt.

THE SWEDISH FURRIER: classic Sherlock Holmes.

THE THIRTEENTH JUROR: crime.

THE WAR EFFORT: humour.

THOSE GHOSTLY VICTORIANS: We are all haunted by dreams…or nightmares. Anthology.

THOSE WICKED WOMEN: adult anthology but not x-rated.

UNTOLD ADVENTURES OF SHERLOCK Holmes: Twelve new Holmes stories.

WITH MALICE AFORETHOUGHT: Sherlock Holmes agrees to protect a man from an unknown enemy, but is the danger real or only imaginary?

WRITTEN IN FIRE: demonic. (May not be suitable for family reading.)

About Me.

For those of you who have not yet made my acquaintance, my name is Annette Siketa and I am totally blind. Were you aware that most blind and visually impaired people are extraordinarily perceptive? To sighted people, this ability must seem like ESP, and I suppose to a certain extent, it is. (I'm referring to the literal meaning of Extra

Sensory Perception and not the spooky interpretation.)

To compensate for the lack of vision, the brain and the other four senses become sharper, so that we can discern a smell or the identity of an object. I promise you, there's no trickery involved. It's simply a matter of adapting the body to 'think' in another way.

Being blind is no barrier to creativity. Like most things in this world, life is what you make of it, and after losing my sight due to an eye operation that went terribly wrong, I became a writer and have now produced a wide variety of books and short stories.

So, how does a blind person write a book? On the practical side, I use a text-to-speech program called 'Jaws', which enables me to use and navigate around a computer, including the Internet, with considerable ease. Information on Jaws can be found at www.freedomscientific.com

On the creative side...well, that's a little more difficult to explain. Try this experiment. Put on your favourite movie and watch it blindfolded. As you already 'know' the movie – who does what where & when etc, your mind compensates for the lack of visualisation by filling in the 'blanks'. Now try it with something you've never seen before - even the six o'clock news. Not so easy to fill in the blanks now, is it?

By this point you're probably going bonkers with frustration – hee hee, welcome to my world! Do not remove the blindfold. Instead, let your imagination compensate for the lack of visualization. This will give you an idea of how I create my stories. Oh, if only Steven Spielberg could read my mind.